Steven George and the Terror

Other Titles by Nathan Everett

STEVEN GEORGE AND THE DRAGON

Steven George is a dragonslayer. He has always known he was a dragonslayer. He was raised to be a dragonslayer. But on the fateful day when he is sent to slay the fiercesome beast, he realizes he doesn't know where the dragon lives, what it looks like, or how to slay it. Thus begins his great adventure, exchanging stories with the people he meets along the way. Each "Once Upon a Time" brings him a step closer to his dragon until Steven realizes that all roads lead to the dragon.

JACKIE THE BEANSTALK

Jackie is a fresh 18-year-old high school graduate, still in her cap and gown when she is given the keys to her grandfather's 1968 Ford Fairlane 500 Fastback. Jackie, Misty, and Roadkill jump in the car and take off on a road trip into an alternate dimension where they encounter robbers, mountain monsters, ogres, obstreperous customs officials, a stowaway princess, an adopted bobcat kitten, werewolves, ghosts, giants, and dragons-all on her way to rescuing the Sovereign's kidnapped son.

A PLACE AT THE TABLE

Though the America Liam Cyning lives in is quite similar to the America of half a century or more ago, it is also fundamentally different. Ten clearly defined classes are the underpinning of American Society, determined by the educational system. As a newly assigned member of the Leader class, Liam is still uncertain what his role and responsibilities are. This story is a Bildungsroman, a literary genre that focuses on the psychological and moral growth of Liam Cyning from youth to adulthood.

CITY LIMITS

Who am I, really? It's a common question. It's part of being self-aware. But is it important? Are we really nothing more than our accumulated lifetime of memories? Or is there something inside that makes us inherently who we are? Stripped of his memories and identity, Gee

Evars must come to grips with who he is as he attempts to make a home among strangers by simply doing the right thing. *City Limits* is the story of Gee's loss of memory and the life and love he gains.

WILD WOODS

When Gee Evars wandered into town, he lost his memory in a daring rescue of a toddler in the raging Rose River. Now the man without a memory has become a force that even the Families need to reckon with. When the city votes to annex South Rosebud, Gee accompanies a small army of high school students to tear down the fence that has separated the cultivated hickory Forest from the Wild Woods. This is where the sequel to the popular novel *City Limits* begins. Gee and his crew must find a way to tame the Wild Woods, uncover its secrets, and live to tell the story. Gee's real work in Rosebud Falls has just begun.

THE GUTENBERG RUBRIC

Two rare-book librarians race across three continents to find and preserve a legendary book printed by Johannes Gutenberg. Behind them, a trail of bombed libraries draws Homeland Security to launch a worldwide search for biblio-terrorists. Keith and Maddie find love along the way, but will they survive to enjoy it?

FOR MONEY OR MAYHEM

Computer forensics detective Dag Hamar has been hired to help a credit card company beef up network security, but are his new co-workers helping him or attacking him? Security video doesn't lie, does it? Dag is about to get dragged from behind his computer screen—away from the comparative safety of cyberspace—into the dirty streets of Seattle where an online predator has become a real-life serial kidnapper. But will he be in time to save his new romance and the daughter who is a victim.

FOR MAYHEM OR MADNESS

Computer forensics detective Dag Hamar is on the case again! In this sequel to *For Money or Mayhem*, Dag is commissioned by the Financial Crimes Enforcement Network (FinCEN) to find and stop a dangerous hacker who appears to be a credible threat to national security. Follow Dag as he erases his own digital identity and goes on the trail around the world to track down and neurtralize Hacker X before he does something really dangerous like erase all the nuclear launch codes in the world. Or maybe, Dag should help him.

FOR BLOOD OR MONEY

DAG HAMAR IS a hard-boiled computer forensics detective with all the trimmings: the Seattle Waterfront office, the sexy young assistant who adores him, and an attitude to match the constant gray drizzle outside his window. And a new missing person case. The only problem is he's a middle-aged computer geek who doesn't do missing persons. And the only clue he has is the missing man's laptop. Dag Hamar and Deb Riley discover hidden files and computer code can be as dangerous as dark alleys and flying bullets as they enter the high-stakes game of of tracing a missing friend and the billion-dollar fortune that disappeared with him.

MUNICIPAL BLONDES

COMPUTER FORENSICS DETECTIVE Deb Riley has been cut loose to continue the work of her partner, Dag Hamar. He sent her to get the code from a dead man's tattoo. He told her she needed to crack the encryption on Simon's thumb drive. He told her he loved her. And then he died. Now Deb finds she is in possession of something everyone wants and will do anything to get. Including kill her. Enter the world of Deb Riley, code breaker, detective, and master of disguise, as she races into the heart of the mystery and risks discovery or worse. She has Dag's reputation to live up to.

STOCKS & BLONDES

COMPUTER FORENSICS DETECTIVE Deb Riley is on the case again, this time with a dead woman named Georgia and a house full of computers. Georgia's father doesn't believe the police finding that she committed suicide. He's sure there was foul play involved. He had no idea how foul it was. Hacking into the computers starts a deadly game as neighbors, friends, and even Georgia, prove not to be what they appear to be. Infiltrating the cabal throws Deb into her deepest disguise ever. Worse, it puts her in danger of ending up just like Georgia.

THE VOLUNTEER

JOURNEY INSIDE THE head of a chronically homeless man--a man that in a less politically correct age we might have called a hobo. Gerald Good, known now only as G2, volunteered to take the place of a homeless man, believing he would work his way back quickly. Ten years later, twenty... thirty years, find G2 alone in his head, his memories, and his boxcar.

"But some day you will be old enough to start

reading fairy tales again."

-C.S. Lewis

Dedication to The Lion, the Witch, and the Wardrobe

THIS BOOK IS dedicated to all those who have learned
that today is our "Once Upon a Time."

Contents

Steven George and the Terror

Nathan Everett

ELDER ROAD BOOKS
LYNNWOOD, WA

1
Passion

TIME IS A FLAME that burns the past as we flee before it to live our lives. We build the flames higher, feeding them with our passions. Sometimes those passions threaten to consume us, and we run faster before the flames that pursue us.

Once in the flames of time, there was a storyteller caught in the passions of his love. He had once been his village's dragonslayer, but the dragon he met was the gypsy Madame Selah Welinska. From their first meeting, Steven George had known that he had met his dragon and she had conquered him. He made his way on the long road with his love, telling and trading stories, sometimes mending and repairing the projects that villagers brought to him. He was not as fine a tinker as the famous Armand Hamar, but it seemed his fires were always hottest and the pots he mended stayed mended.

But as time passed, the lovers' passion increased, so that it threatened to consume them. Not only did they love passionately, but they fought passionately as well. When Steven looked into Selah's eyes, it was hard not to see the green vertical slits of the dragon he had once mastered. At times, he felt so hot that he feared he would burst into flames. Lately, it seemed every decision in their unconstrained lives was cause for conflict.

It was this, in fact, that brought the couple to their current campsite. The patient little donkey, Xandros, who willingly pulled their meager possessions in a cart, had come to a fork in the road and had stopped, waiting for the couple to tell him which way to turn. He would have followed directions from either, but neither could agree on the direction to take. Steven stood on the left path, while Selah stood on the right path, shouting at each other about the merits of which way their journey should take them.

"It is too cold to go north into the mountains," Selah stated matter-of-factly, in a voice that could be heard a mile down either path.

"The path into the forest provides shelter, food, and firewood," Steven responded in a voice that made the donkey cringe.

Selah scuffed in the dirt with her bare heel and proudly pointed at the ground. "The yellow brick road goes this way," she said. "I follow the long road and the bricklayer Xandros has paved it with bricks."

Somewhat dismayed by this bit of news, Steven scuffed at the road on which he stood and spoke up sharply. "The bricklayer has been this way as well," he said pointing at the yellow bricks paving his road. "We should follow the road the bricklayer laid into the forest."

"You traded for warm clothes in the village a week ago while I was in the hills. I am still barefoot."

"You generate enough heat to keep the whole forest warm."

The argument proceeded without pause for over an hour, until both were hoarse with shouting. All this while the little donkey—named for the famous bricklayer who built the long road—stood at the fork, swinging his head from one side to the other. Left fork? Right fork? Finally, he sat down in the traces and began to bray.

Steven and Selah stopped their argument, which had brought them closer and closer at the fork. They looked at the little donkey, and then they looked at each other, and then they began to laugh. Without saying another word, Selah unhitched Xandros—named after the famous bricklayer—and set him free to graze. Steven gathered wood and built a fire pit surrounded by stones. Before the sun went down, the two sprawled together next to the fire, eating the burnt bits of a rabbit that Steven had snared while the donkey grazed quietly nearby. The argument forgotten for the moment, they laughed as they tore bits of meat from the bones and fed them to each other.

Steven rose to tend to the donkey and rub him down, much to the little beast's delight, as Selah banked the fires. Soon Steven heard the ring of finger cymbals that he had learned meant his love was beginning to dance.

He returned to the fire where Selah had begun to beat out a gentle tempo with her feet in time to the cymbals. He pulled his little bone whistle from his belt and began to improvise a tune to go with the increasingly complex rhythm that she beat. From a slow and deliberate pace to a moderate whirl to a spinning dance that would collapse a dervish, the dance picked up speed and passion, fanning the banked fires with the breeze it created. At last, the tempo could no longer be sustained, and the gypsy woman fell into the arms of her lover. They collapsed in giggles, panting for air. Steven drew Selah to him in a kiss, but she pushed him away.

"Not yet, Steven George, dragonslayer," she laughed. "I want to tell a story."

"Do you mean to once upon a time me?" he asked.

"Once or twice or as often as you like," she said, chuckling at an old joke between the two. "But you must return with a story of your own. I am already one ahead of you and you owe me. I want to know the story of your new sheepskin vest."

Steven patted the wool of the garment. He had acquired it at the last village, but not in the way Selah thought.

"Perhaps you would like me to go first?" he asked.

"No," she answered. "I really don't mind you owing me one."

And so, they lay down on their bedrolls beneath the stars and Madame Selah Welinska began her story.

2
The Fool's Gold

ONCE UPON A TIME, there was a tiny gnome named Fonrick, who lived beneath the rugged garden wall of a great castle. He had enjoyed his position in the royal gardens for many years and had seen several generations of kings come to the throne. He had always maintained a good standing with the rulers of this little kingdom. The kitchen staff depended on him to scout out the best vegetables for the king's table. Fonrick was comfortable and fat and raised a lovely little family of gnomes over the years.

It was this, in fact, that proved to be the source of Fonrick's problems. When the little gnome's youngest son, Nerrick, was just a hundred summers old, he set out to find his own garden in the world. Just as he was setting up a new home at a small cottage he had found, a crotchety old gardener named Haruld discovered him. Haruld was of the school that considered garden gnomes to be common pests, and was determined to drown Nerrick. In fear for his life, Nerrick began begging and ultimately arrived at reciting his family heritage and lineage. When Haruld heard that Nerrick's family lived beneath the wall of the castle gardens, the cagey old man hesitated.

"Ah," he thought. "Perhaps this little gnome could have his uses."

He placed Nerrick in a bucket and put a plank over it while he contemplated the possibilities, for if Haruld was anything more than a crotchety old man, he was a greedy old man. He sat at his table eating stale bread and drinking sour wine, with his feet propped on top of the bucket, and mused aloud.

"I suppose that being raised in the castle, you are wealthy," he began. Nerrick was silent while listening. "Your family, I suppose, are still living at the castle and would hate to see anything happen to their little gnome-let," he continued. "They would probably pay some of the king's gold to keep little Nerrick from harm. Now if that gold were to find its way to me, I might be persuaded to let this little gnome stay in my garden. What do you say, little gnome? Will you be my hostage for ransom, or will you die in my well?"

Now Nerrick was truly panicked, for although his family was happy and had all they needed, they had never needed gold. They ate from the king's garden and the king's cook left them special sweets. Their home beneath the garden wall was snug and comfortable. None of Nerrick's family in all their years had needed gold. But the little gnome knew that if he did not agree to the terms, he would be drowned in the well.

"Perhaps," he thought, "if I agree to these terms, I might find a way to escape."

"Oh, great and mighty master," answered Nerrick. "If I could just go to my family, I would take your demands and bring you the gold you seek. Then we could live in peace and harmony in your garden."

"What do you take me for, gnome?" huffed the old man. "If I let you go, you would never come back, and I would have neither gold nor the pleasure of drowning you! I shall take you on a leash to the home of your parents and we shall make the demands together."

With that, the greedy gardener fashioned a small leash out of an old leather satchel. He took the board off the bucket and, before Nerrick could gasp for breath, had the leash fastened around the gnome's neck.

The poor gnome was led thus to the castle walls and in his humiliation was forced to call out to his family.

"Father, father," Nerrick cried. "Your son has come to visit. Please come outside the castle wall to speak with me."

Not knowing what had happened to his son, Fonrick slipped through his back door to see why he had been called. When he saw his son with a leash around his neck he was filled with fury.

"What is the meaning of this? Why have you shackled my son and brought him thus to my door?" Fonrick demanded.

"Your son trespassed on my property," said Haruld. "I have come to demand ransom for him. You must bring me five gold pieces or I shall drown your son in my well."

"And if I bring you gold?" asked Fonrick, smelling a foul odor in the man's offer.

"Why then, of course, he will live beneath my garden wall as a free, rent-paying tenant," responded Haruld.

Now, neither Fonrick nor Haruld, nor even Nerrick believed for a moment that Nerrick would be free, for the desire for gold is a disease that consumes the heart, and Haruld had contracted the disease when Nerrick first mentioned the castle. But Fonrick had not lived to the age of 832 summers without gaining some knowledge and proving that he was clever enough to survive. So, he answered the gardener.

"It shall be as you have demanded," said Fonrick, chuckling.

"What do you find so funny?" demanded Haruld. Nerrick was terrified.

"Why, that you demand so little," answered Fonrick. "Here you have captured a gnome of the king's household and yet all you want is a few pieces of gold."

This truly gave Haruld pause. In his very small mind, five pieces of gold seemed like a king's ransom. And, indeed, it was more by far than Fonrick actually possessed. But it started the greedy old man thinking. If the gnome was worth five gold coins, of course, he would be worth ten gold coins. And everyone knows that to a king, twenty gold coins are no more noticeable than ten. If he could get twenty gold coins from the king, why couldn't he get fifty? Or even…

"I demand one hundred gold coins ransom for this royal gnome's ransom," boldly declared Haruld the gardener.

Everywhere he looked, he could see gold. He imagined himself riding down the street on his proud horse, graciously tossing copper coins to the peasants who bowed before him. He would build himself a new house and a larger garden and enslave thousands of gnomes to tend it so he would never have to work again. All this flashed through his mind as Fonrick's eyes squinted shut. The gardener saw the expression and knew he had gotten the best of the gnome family. In fact, Fonrick was trying hard to control his laughter. At last, he was able to open his eyes and calmly address Haruld.

"You have the best of me, master gardener," said Fonrick. "Indeed, I would pay any sum to save my son, but for such a man as you, I would do even more. Your wisdom and shrewdness have brought me to conclude that you yourself should rule the kingdom."

This startled Haruld even more, but the idea instantly took root in his mind. He pictured himself sleeping in the castle with waiters bringing food and wine for him.

"Indeed, I should," he bragged. "But first I must have gold."

"I can show you where there is more gold than the mind can fathom. I have lived in this garden for eight centuries, and I have watched the kings carefully. They are all fools. For generations they have stashed their gold and precious jewels in a cave on the other side of the mountain. Unknown to them, I have stowed away in their wagons on nights under the dark moon when they visited their treasure trove. The king lives in poverty here compared to what he could have. He could pave the streets in gold and sleep on a golden bed, drive a golden carriage, and eat from golden plates. All this with the gold in that treasury. And I will show you where this treasure is stored."

Haruld sat back on the ground grasping his heart. His cunning had paid off. He would be unimaginably rich. Then he would drown this gnome and all the others in his family so there would be no witness to his theft. It remained only to follow Fonrick to the king's treasure cave.

Now, Fonrick was 832 summers old and had not always lived under the garden wall of the castle. For a gnome, he had traveled far and seen strange things. One of those things was a dragon. He had followed the trail of the dragon for weeks until he had found it asleep in its cave high above the river valley on the other side of the mountain. There he had seen the dragon's vast wealth, gathered into a nest on which the dragon slept at night.

But Fonrick was a gnome, not a dwarf. He had little or no interest in such wealth. The adventure of seeing a dragon was all the reward that he wanted for his efforts.

And so, he had told no one about the dragon and its cave of riches in all these hundreds of years.

He advised the gardener to bring his wagon and cart-horse to the city gate the next morning. Fonrick and his son would show Haruld the way to the cave of riches. Haruld was just canny enough to think at the last minute that he had better keep Nerrick securely in hand until the wealth had been delivered, so the poor boy soon found himself back in the bucket as Haruld slept with his feet on the board.

The next morning Fonrick met his son and the gardener at the city gates, and they set out for the mountain. It was a long journey, but Fonrick kept Haruld's interest by giving him details of the kind of wealth they would find. At long last, they reached the cave. Haruld lit a torch and proceeded inside. All was silent. As soon as they were deep in the cave, the light of the torch fell upon the gold. Even Fonrick's tales had not prepared the gardener for such a sight. He waded into gold vessels, plates, coins, and jewelry up to his waist. He bathed in his prize and laughed insanely, throwing gold up over his head and letting it rain down upon him. At long last, exhausted by his celebration, Haruld collapsed on the piled wealth and fell fast asleep.

As soon as he was asleep, Fonrick freed his son and led him quietly away from the cave and back down the mountain the way they had come.

As the moon rose, they saw the silhouette of a dragon winging across the skies, headed toward the cave. No one knows if the dragon killed the foolish gardener when he was found on the hoard. Perhaps there was no dragon and Haruld went mad refusing to leave the treasure again. Or, perhaps while lying on the dragon's nest of gold, thinking dragonish thoughts, the greedy fool was transformed into the dragon himself.

But of this people are agreed: Travelers along the river below hear insane laughter in the middle of the night and swear the echo calls "Gold! Gold!" But none who have ever sought for the treasure have returned to tell their tale.

3
Soldier

IN THE MORNING, they had still not determined which direction they were to go, but before they could begin arguing about the matter, the stillness of the country was broken by a whistled tune. Xandros the donkey was the first to hear it and alerted the couple with his bray. The tune was not a merry tune, nor particularly sad. It was a tune punctuated by measured footsteps tramping on the path through the forest. The tune was a marching tune.

"Now, here comes a reason to have taken the south path," Steven muttered under his breath.

Selah smiled smugly as they awaited the approach of the marchers. Soon three soldiers marched into view and came to a halt at the edge of Steven's camp. The leading soldier walked directly up to Steven.

"Are you Steven George the Dragonslayer?" he asked gruffly.

A truly clever and quick-witted man might have made up another name on the spot, but Steven was not clever and quick-witted enough to lie to the soldier.

"I am Steven George, sometimes called Dragonslayer, but the truth is that I didn't really…"

"Doesn't matter," said the soldier. "Never met a dragon. Never want to. It's just a name."

The fire where Steven had been cooking breakfast suddenly flared to life, startling the soldiers. Steven spared a glance at Selah who smiled demurely.

"Well, how can I help you?" Steven asked.

"Steven George the Dragonslayer," intoned the sergeant in his best heraldic voice, "you are summoned to the presence of Montague Magnus the Fourth, King and Liege of Sylgale, Puissant Paragon of Mariria, and the Simple Pride of Arining, to dine at the King's table and regale our monarch with tales of your adventures; for which His Royal Highness has promised you just compensation and opportunity for magnanimous reward."

The sergeant then turned to look at his two men, who briefly consulted with each other and then nodded back to the sergeant. It was obvious that the poor soldier was not used to delivering decrees from the King and had been practicing on his comrades in arms for as long as they had been on the road.

Agreed that he had delivered the message correctly, the soldiers began to sniff the air.

"Is that a stew cooking on your fire?" asked the sergeant hungrily.

"It is," said Selah coming forward. "We had rabbit for dinner and made the rest into a stew this morning. Would you care to join us?"

As hungrily as the men gazed toward the fire, the sergeant still demurred.

"Now, we couldn't eat rabbits that were poached from the King's lands," he said. "It's a crime and you may be punished when the King is told. We have rations we can eat."

"Really?" asked Selah. "And where are the King's lands?"

"Oh, all this forest is the King's," said the sergeant. "Anything caught within it is his."

"Well, that settles it," Selah said with finality. "These rabbits were caught in the field here, not within the King's forest. Surely now you can join us to eat." The soldiers consulted with each other quietly, then the sergeant turned again to Madame Selah Welinska and bowed.

"Seeing as no rabbits were caught in the King's forest, there can be no harm in our accepting your invitation, Lady. We would be most delighted to dine with you," he said as respectfully as possible. "And there need be no report or mention of what didn't happen should any soldier appear before the King, neither."

With that the soldiers dropped their packs and disassembled their mess kits, standing at attention in line next to the fire as Selah dished out stew. They fell to eating with the appetite of soldiers on a long march. When they were scraping out the bottom of their plates, one of the other soldiers—who looked as much like the other as twins—spoke to Selah.

"Begging your pardon, lady," he said to her. "But would you be the dragon-lady spoken of in so many stories?"

The sergeant rapped the young soldier on the head and reprimanded him sharply for his impudence. Therefore, none of the soldiers noticed the fiery look that Selah gave to Steven.

"So, I'm spoken of in many stories, am I?" she began. "Pray tell, what do these stories say?"

"Well, now, 'many' is a relative term. When a man has heard only two, one is many of them. And that was just hearsay. The boy meant no insult, Madame," said the sergeant. "We were given specific instructions on how to identify the dragonslayer. We were told that he travels in the company of a beautiful lady that was sometimes called the dragon-lady. Personally, I never met nobody who would dare to call her that to her face. It was of no more significance than the mention of a donkey. It was how we were told to identify Steven George the Dragonslayer."

"And does the King's summons extend to the dragon-lady and the donkey?"

"I ain't saying they wouldn't be welcomed in the court, but the King made no mention of inviting the lady and the donkey. Not that the King would ever presume on her nor neglect to mention her. 'Twas an urgent summons for the Dragonslayer only."

"Good," she said with finality that startled Steven. He could not mistake the fact that she looked determinedly down the southbound road.

"We should start back," the soldier said. "If you would be so kind as to accompany us, Steven George the Dragonslayer?"

Steven was not ready to make this decision. He could see that Madame Selah Welinska was still determined to travel south. He needed to have time to convince her to go with him.

"How many steps is it to the King's court?" Steven asked the sergeant.

"How many steps?" the sergeant asked. "Now I don't rightly know. It is three days' march back the way we came through the forest."

"Three days and you cannot kill any game to eat?" Steven asked.

"We have rations."

"I don't," Steven continued. "What do you say we spend the day hunting here in the prairie fields where there is an abundance of rabbits and an occasional deer? Then we can prepare roast meats for the journey tomorrow."

"That sounds all right," said one of the soldiers. Steven could not tell if it was the one who had spoken before.

"Now, just a minute," said the sergeant. "We need to get the message to the King that the Dragonslayer is approaching. Otherwise, half the soldiers in the kingdom will continue to be out on the road looking for him."

"Are more looking for me than you?" Steven asked incredulously.

"Oh yes, sir," said the sergeant. "The first ones went out two weeks ago. We were sent out just a few days ago. They are searching in every direction for you. I'm not saying they aren't searching the south road as well."

Steven contemplated what this might mean, as the sergeant turned to his men.

"Now you two will have to double-time back to the castle and I will stay and escort this party back at their pace. Our orders was to treat them kindly, but we have got to get word back. You two got full bellies now, so get going. You should be able to get there by nightfall tomorrow and tell them to get things ready."

There was considerable grumbling, and at last Selah packed the men a few strips of dried venison from their stores and told them how to make a savory stew out of it. Soon the two were gone.

"Wouldn't one of them have traveled back faster than two?" asked Steven.

"Soldiers don't travel alone," said the sergeant. "I'm not saying they're simple, but it takes both of those two to equal one good man."

"But that means you are alone," said Steven.

"No, not exactly," said the sergeant. "I'm with you."

"But I may not choose to go to the King's court,"

Steven said.

"Now, I can't force you to come to the King's banquet table," said the sergeant. "You are not presently under arrest. I'm merely here to escort you and protect you from the forest bandits. So, if you choose not to go to the King, then I'll just have to go with you."

Selah snorted next to the wagon in a very unladylike way. Steven decided that it was best to get the sergeant out in the field hunting rather than talking in camp.

"I found the rabbits just at that rise," he said. "Why don't you go set a couple of traps and I'll get my bow."

He winked at the sergeant and nodded over his shoulder toward Selah as if to indicate that he wanted time alone with her. In a trice, the sergeant perceived his meaning and said loudly that he would be just "over there," where Steven could join him. He was no more than out of earshot when Steven turned to Selah.

"Don't even ask," said Selah as Steven opened his mouth. "I will not be traveling the north road to a walled castle through the lands of a king who thinks the free game of the world is his personal property. You go and pay homage or be honored or whatever the mad monarch wants. We'll meet up again later."

"Where and when will we meet, Madame?" asked Steven. "How will I ever find you again?"

"How did you find me the first time?" answered the dragon-lady. "One day I will be in your path and you will find me."

"When?"

"Steven, how long have we traveled together?" asked Selah.

"Thousands of steps over many seasons," Steven answered.

"You must learn to tell time and distance like other people," Selah laughed. "It has been seven years. It seems like it would be a good idea to travel our own roads for a time and see if we still like each other."

"Like each other?" asked Steven. "But I love you!"

"Then our love should be stronger when we meet again."

"But I will be an old man," Steven lamented.

"Look at you, Steven George the Dragonslayer," Selah laughed. "You are younger now than when we first met. At this rate, if we stayed together, you would be in a short tunic playing with colored stones. Being apart, maybe you will be as old as you were when we met the first time!"

"I shall always miss you and mourn our parting," Steven said.

"You shall always wonder if I ever really existed or was just a dream," Selah smiled. "Ah, Steven, it is truly better if we walk our own paths for a while before we kill each other. Have you not noticed how hot our arguments have become? This time of cooling off will do us both great good. Now go help your poor soldier capture a rabbit or there will be no supper."

"If I turn, you will leave," Steven said.

"Not before you tell me about your vest," she answered. "Remember?"

Steven kissed Selah, Then he turned, retrieved his bow from the wagon, and went to hunt with the sergeant.

AFTER THEY HAD cleaned the game and feasted on a roast haunch of venison with the remainder smoking over the fire pit, Selah began to dance. The sergeant was rapt with the hypnotic movements of the dance. Selah's gestures wove a spell that held even Steven speechless for a time. But for the soldier, the trance was deep, and when she stopped dancing, he began to snore.

"Now," said Selah to Steven as she snuggled into his arms, "about that one you owe me."

4
The Inevitable Change

ONCE UPON A TIME, there was a midwife. We assume she was given a name when she was born as most babies are, but over the years she had adopted the name of her patroness as many in that profession do, and was called Mylitta of the Green Vale. Throughout the valley, children had found their way into the world at her coaxing, and mothers had survived the most rigorous childbirths because of her care.

Mylitta was the first of twelve children, herself. From the time she was just upright on two feet, she had been with her mother at the birthing of a child. And when it was not her mother giving birth, her mother was helping a neighbor give birth or even helping the livestock in the barn. Mylitta had been around birth all her life.

Mylitta was at the birth of her sister, four brothers, two more sisters, a brother, two more sisters, and a brother. She watched her neighbor give birth to her firstborn with her mother in attendance. She helped with the calving in the spring at her father's side, and sat with newborns through the night to be sure they suckled and were not rejected. When she was ten years old, Mylitta and her mother were called to the home of the magistrate of the nearest city where the magistrate's wife, Ell, was in the midst of a particularly difficult birth. Mylitta rushed to get bowls of hot and cold water, fresh clean cloths, and to organize the servants to instantly carry out orders as they were needed.

When she returned to her mother, she was asked to help support Ell as her mother positioned the birthing bed beneath her. It seemed remarkable to Mylitta that as soon as Ell rested upon the old fleece, her breathing eased, and her desperation seemed to disappear. Ell smiled weakly at Mylitta.

"How nice that my little daughter will have a sister to welcome her into the world," Ell breathed weakly. "Just having you here makes the labor easier." It was not long after that Mylitta's mother reached into Ell's womb and turned the baby, so the little girl was born headfirst into the world. Ell, though weak, smiled and brought the babe to her breast, then fell asleep at last.

"Mother," said Mylitta quietly, "it was not really my presence that comforted Ell, was it?"

"Sweet child," said her mother, "your presence is always a comfort to mothers—even to me. But you are right in assuming it is not just your presence. It is the property of the birthing bed to bring change upon those who rest in its embrace. For you see, daughter, this old fleece is enchanted."

The birthing bed had been present through every birth that Mylitta had attended. Her mother even threw it over the backs of cows, sows, and ewes when they experienced hard births. Though it was called a bed, it was nothing more than a huge sheepskin that Mylitta and her mother placed beneath the birthing woman to welcome her child. It was soft and was always cleaned with tropical oil and treated with wool wax. It was impervious to any stains.

"This sacred birthing bed…" Mylitta's mother told her, "…has seen the births of kings and queens in ages past. It was the object of an ancient quest and is made from the skin of the prized ewe of Aciannis, goddess of health in ancient Ursentia. The ewe gave birth to the stars and in her old age was sacrificed to save the life of Aciannis's own child. Since that time, it has been passed down from generation to generation. This, I am told, is but a fragment of the original fleece, which has been divided among midwives the world over."

MYLITTA WAS IN her twentieth winter when her mother gave birth to the last of the children. After Mylitta had cleaned the sheepskin and brushed it with wool wax, she gave it to her mother while watching her newest little brother suckle. She was surprised when her mother handed the heirloom back.

"It is for you, now, child," her mother said. "I will have no more children. You will take this wherever you go and protect the newborns and their mothers with it."

"But mother," Mylitta said, "I have no husband and no desire to get one. Give it instead to one of your daughters who will marry."

Mylitta's mother laughed a little at this, jostling the suckling infant. She well understood that the girl had seen enough of childbirth to shrink at the thought of becoming pregnant herself. But she also saw how talented her daughter was at helping in the process.

"You may not wish for children of your own, my dear," said her mother, "but those who do will want you at their side. Take it and share its comfort with those in need." Mylitta took the skin as her mother instructed her, but her mother was not finished yet. "Always remember, whoever lies upon the birthing bed changes forever."

MANY YEARS PASSED and Mylitta became a legendary midwife. But then a great plague came on the land. People were sick in every town and farm, and many died. No children were being born, but Mylitta was kept busy tending the sick. These, too, seemed comforted by the birthing bed, and many were borne into the spirit world while resting on it.

The last victim of the plague was Mylitta herself. She came home from tending the last of the ill and lay down. She was so tired that she fell asleep on top of the birthing bed that had welcomed her into this world. She dreamt of her mother and of all the babies she had welcomed into the world on this very fleece. And she saw the spirits of the dead welcomed into their new lives while lying on the old sheepskin. And then she knew the truth of the legend her mother had told her. Whatever lay upon the sheepskin changed, but so did everything else in the world.

It is said that Mylitta's laughter is what drew the only witness to her death that day. And Mylitta pushed the sheepskin into the hands of the visitor with her last breath, saying "She changes everything she touches and everything she touches changes."

Not knowing the story behind the sheepskin, the unnamed visitor thought at first to burn it for fear that the plague was in the sheepskin. But it was so soft and pleasant to the touch that she kept it, washed it carefully, and waxed the wool. Then, not knowing what else to do with it, she thought how it could keep her warm in the winter. She cut it and sewed it into a vest, mittens, and a liner for her boots that she wore all through the winter months.

By the end of the winter, however, she realized that there were those less fortunate than her and she gave the vest to a traveler and the mittens to a child. The boots she wore until her own death, and they were passed on as well. All through her life she was known as a kind and giving woman who helped the poor and provided for the needy.

The traveler who had received the vest stopped traveling and began to farm. Since he was no longer on the road and had a comfortable house to live in, he gave the vest to another, and so it happened that the vest has come down in this way to me. It is the vest of Mylitta, and protects me from harm. But all those who have worn it have changed, and now, so have I. For where I once traveled the long road with my love, now I set foot on it alone.

And one day, I shall pass it on to a traveler that I meet.

<h1 style="text-align:center">5
Forest</h1>

WHEN STEVEN WOKE in the morning, he was cold like he could not remember being in all the time he had traveled with Selah. He rolled over, but she was not next to him. Rubbing sleep from his eyes he sat up and looked around. A few steps away, a soldier stood as if on guard, gazing out toward the south.

Ah, yes, Steven thought. *The sergeant.*

Then Steven took in the rest of the campsite. The fire still smoldered, and his pack lay at his head. But there was no sign of Selah. Or the donkey. Or the wagon. He rubbed his eyes and looked around again, scrambling out of his bedroll. He rushed to the sergeant.

"Where is Selah?" he demanded of the soldier.

"Who is Selah?" responded the sergeant.

"Selah is my... The lady who was with me when you found us yesterday. And the donkey and cart?" Steven blurted.

"I don't know about no lady, sir," said the sergeant calmly. "There is no lady here, nor donkey and cart, neither."

"I can see she is not here," said Steven, "but where is she?"

"Now how would I be supposed to know that?" asked the sergeant. "If there is no lady here, why would I know where the lady is? You are not making sense, sir, if I may be so plain."

"Now see here," Steven blustered. "Yesterday you arrived with two other soldiers and found Madame Selah Welinska, Xandros the donkey, my cart, and me. You sent the other two back to court to tell the King I'd been found. We spent the day hunting and preparing supplies for the journey through the King's forest. We ate dinner and Selah danced and you fell asleep. Now where is Madame Welinska?"

"Well, now, that is just as I remember things," said the sergeant. "But I'm not committing to having seen a lady. No, I can't say that I did."

Steven was dumbfounded. The soldier was aggravating. What did he mean by not committing to having seen a lady after he just agreed that she'd been there and danced the night before? Steven had slept in her arms until… He wasn't quite sure exactly when, but he had fallen asleep in her arms. And he had been traveling with the blasted little donkey and cart for seven years. He began to look on the ground for tracks indicating which way they had gone.

He found none.

As far as Steven could tell by the ground, there had been no one camped in this hollow but him and the soldier. There were no donkey tracks or other signs. There were no wagon ruts. There was nothing that would indicate anything other than what the sergeant had said.

Steven sat in the middle of the road and ground the heels of his palms into his eyes. He scuffed his feet into the dirt of the road looking for a sign of bricks, but even that evaded his investigation. Steven was heartbroken and confused. It was not possible that he had been here alone. What had transpired over the past seven years?

"Now, begging your pardon, sir," interrupted the sergeant, "If you wouldn't mind getting your pack together, we could get under way. Our journey lies that way," he said pointing into the forest.

"Yes. Certainly," Steven said quietly. He silently got up and put his pack together. There were plenty of strips of roast venison to pack in his bag, but certainly not a whole deer worth. He supposed it was just as well that Selah had taken the rest of the meat, because without the wagon he would surely have no means to transport it. He still could not understand how he could have slept through Selah rising, harnessing the donkey, and pulling the wagon with its tinkling bells away from the camp.

At last, he shouldered his pack, picked up his walking stick, and looked sadly around the last campsite he'd shared with his beloved.

"Are you absolutely sure you didn't wake up when the lady left?" he asked the sergeant.

"Now, a soldier is always alert to what is going on, son," said the sergeant. "I ain't saying I slept the whole night long, but I ain't saying I saw no lady get up and spirit away a donkey and wagon in the middle of the night, neither."

"Spirit away? You mean she just vanished?" Steven asked incredulously.

"I didn't say I saw that," said the sergeant. "You can't convict me for something I didn't confess to. Now if we could get moving?"

"Lead on," Steven growled.

He followed the soldier into the forest.

THEY HAD NOT gone far into the forest when Steven began to feel the need to talk. He had begun counting steps the moment they left the campsite—something he had not done in seven years. But now it seemed that if he kept track of the footsteps, he would know how far and in what direction he needed to go to get back to his beloved Madame Selah Welinska. The footsteps seemed hollow, however, and he was sure he could entice the sergeant to tell him more.

"Sergeant," said Steven finally, "I don't know your name. I am Steven George the Storyteller. What are you called?"

"I'm called Sergeant by those who know what's good for them," he answered.

"But surely you have a name, don't you?" Steven probed.

"I ain't saying I don't have a name," the sergeant answered. "You asked what I'm called. I'm called Sergeant."

"All right, Sergeant," Steven continued. "What is your name?"

The sergeant mumbled something in return and Steven asked him to repeat it.

"Busker," the sergeant said more loudly. "I'm Sergeant Busker, if you must know. Now can we pick up the pace a bit here?"

"Well, Busker," said Steven, "shall we tell each other stories to make the journey go faster?"

"Sergeant," answered Sergeant Busker. "No one calls me Busker. And if you would like to make the journey go faster, we could pick up the pace a bit. This scarcely quali-fies as a march."

"I didn't know we were marching," Steven said.

"Soldiers march," Busker answered.

"I'm not a soldier. I'm a storyteller," Steven said. "I walk. So far, we have come seven thousand two hundred fifty-five steps this morning."

"I'm a soldier. I march," Sergeant answered. "We have barely 'walked' a league."

It had been many years since Steven had picked up the pace, as Sergeant wanted. He had never hurried anywhere since meeting Madame Welinska seven years ago. But he remembered the one hundred five step-per-minute pace that had always been his norm on the road and determined to regain it for the sake of having civil conversation with Sergeant.

Sergeant was pleased when Steven set out a longer stride, but Steven had difficulty maintaining a consistent pace. *It was once so simple,* he thought. *How I have changed.*

"Why don't you Once Upon a Time me," Steven asked presently.

"I beg your pardon?" Sergeant shot at him.

"Tell me a story," Steven clarified. "Then I shall tell you a story. It will be a pleasant way to pass the time and we shall both be a story richer by the end of the day."

"Soldiers don't tell stories," Sergeant retorted. "Soldiers say only what they see with their own two eyes. Soldiers must always be depended upon to report accurately to their superior officers."

"Well, let's start there then," Steven said happily. "What did you see with your own two eyes when you woke up in the middle of the night just before the lady and the donkey vanished."

"I ain't saying I saw no lady in the middle of the night," said Sergeant. "I ain't saying I saw no great winged dragon launch into the sky with a baby dragon at its side and a wagon in its claws, neither. That would be a silly thing to say I saw. No one would never believe it."

"You saw a what?" Steven gasped.

"I didn't say I saw nothing," Sergeant said firmly and set his jaw as he lengthened his stride. Steven found himself running to catch up, walking and falling behind, and running again as the soldier seemed to maintain a smooth even stride. Sergeant finally pulled a small tambour from his pack and began tapping out the pace for their march. Steven found it much easier to settle into the pace with the steady beat.

"Is this how a soldier marches?" Steven asked after his breathing had caught up with the new pace.

"Aye, it is," said Sergeant. "I use this to help new recruits learn how to set an even pace."

"Tell me more about being a soldier," Steven begged after they had traveled two more leagues, as Sergeant call them. The path which had once been a road continued to narrow, and they now "marched" in single file.

"What do you want to know?" asked Sergeant.

"I know nothing about the life of a soldier," said Steven. "We have passed soldiers at different times, but never talked to them. I once served a company of knights. Is being a soldier like being a knight?"

"No!" answered Sergeant emphatically. "Being a soldier is more like being a knight's horse, except you aren't cared for so well."

"Oh," Steven said as he thought about how the company of knights had cared for their horses. The horses were always cooled, watered, fed, and brushed before the knights sat to eat. "Tell me more about being a soldier."

"You want to know about being a soldier?" Sergeant asked.

"Yes," said Steven. "Tell me about being a soldier."

"Duck," Sergeant said matter-of-factly.

"Wha…?" Steven began as the branch Sergeant had pushed out of the way snapped back and struck Steven full in the face, knocking him to the ground.

"That's one," Sergeant said, offering Steven a hand to get up to his feet. "A soldier obeys orders instantly. This time it was just a branch in your face. Next time it could be your life on the line."

Steven climbed to his feet rubbing his face and mouth where the branch had struck.

"Now, step lively, recruit," barked Sergeant, as he began a rapid tattoo on the tambour. Steven found it much easier to keep the pace now as he was alert to any sign that Sergeant would snap another branch into his face. The forest became denser, and the path got even narrower.

"Is the road like this all the way through the forest?" Steven asked. He was already regretting having ever argued with Selah about what direction they should go. The donkey and cart could never have made it through this dense undergrowth. *Baby dragon?* he thought fleetingly. *Where had the road gone?*

"We're taking a shortcut," said Sergeant. "We left the road two leagues ago. This path is a little more rugged, but we'll get to the castle a full day earlier if we keep up this pace."

Steven was listening to Sergeant, but even more to the forest sounds around him. In all his travels since he crossed the great river near his village, he had never left the road. It seemed to go everywhere he and Selah wanted to go. This was more rugged than even the game trails near the home he had left so long ago.

The sounds were different here. Sergeant had left off tapping the tambour as the forest closed in. Now, Steven was aware of his own heavy breathing and more than once thought he heard breathing behind him. He kept as close as he could to Sergeant, and thought the soldier had also become increasingly alert.

"Double time," Sergeant said suddenly, and broke into a trot. Steven did not hesitate to keep pace as the forest seemed to become more and more threatening. The sun had been blocked completely by the foliage and Steven was certain he heard branches snapping behind and beside him.

Something was on their trail, and Steven wanted nothing more than to string his bow and nock an arrow. Sweat trickled down his forehead and into his eyes as he stumbled suddenly into a small clearing at the edge of a cliff. Without hesitating, Sergeant went over the edge, commanding, "Jump!"

Steven hesitated. Was he mad? He turned to look behind him and was faced with the biggest bear he had ever imagined. So startled was Steven that he stepped backward and over the edge of the cliff.

Time stopped as Steven saw the bear charge toward him, only to slide to a halt at the edge of the cliff, watching his dinner fall into the void. It seemed forever, as Steven held the eyes of the bear receding into the distance. Then his fall was arrested by tree limbs, giving way to dense brush that cushioned his impact with the ground that he never quite touched before stopping.

"Hoo-woo!" shouted Sergeant, jumping on the springy undergrowth. He offered Steven a hand and pulled him to his feet as they stepped off the cushion at the foot of the cliff and onto a path again.

"We jumped off a cliff!" Steven shouted in disbelief.

"Always trust your sergeant, recruit," said Sergeant. "He'll never lead you astray."

"You knew we'd bounce?" Steven asked.

"It's not like I've never done this before," Busker said, "but I'm not saying I have, either. We usually take the path down the cliff over there," he said pointing. "Speaking of which, we should get a good distance between us and this cliff, just in case that old bear decides we're worth coming down the path for. If we'd tried to come down that way, one or both of us would have been dinner. But at least it was just a big old bear and not the Terror."

Steven was shaking as they set off down the path again. The going became easier on this side of the cliff and by late in the afternoon they reached a river.

"We'll camp here," said Sergeant. "We've come nearly halfway to the castle now and the way will be easier after we cross the river."

"Wouldn't it be safer to cross the river now?" asked Steven. "We could be on the opposite side of where the bear is."

"Oh, the bear is long behind us now," Sergeant laughed. "Besides, a little thing like a river would be no barrier to it. Bears can swim. We'll have to be careful to pick our way across on the rocks and I'd rather do that in the light of the morning, with a full belly and a night's rest."

They built a fire and enjoyed the venison they had packed. Steven was exhausted from the forced march of the day and could not remember the last time he had covered forty-two thousand seven hundred forty steps in a day. He surprised himself with that. Even running from the bear and jumping—or falling—off the cliff had not interrupted his count. He still knew where to go to get back to Selah.

HE SLEPT FITFULLY through the night, thinking at every moment that he heard the bear coming through the woods. But nothing appeared near the fire. In the morning, they continued their journey and at long last Steven saw the largest city he had seen since leaving Byzantium years ago. It was an uncomfortable feeling, for Steven's adventures in the city had been disastrous, leaving without his knife, sword, horse, bow, or coins. There was little to be done, however, and he resolutely followed Sergeant into the castle of the King.

6
King

STEVEN AND SERGEANT arrived at the castle and the busy metropolis that surrounded it just minutes after the twin soldiers the sergeant had sent ahead arrived to announce they were coming. The soldiers had taken the road through the forest instead of the shortcut, and still managed to get lost on the way home. As a result, no one was ready for Steven's sudden arrival. He was treated as an obstacle in the way, as the castle prepared for "an important guest," and thought perhaps he had been summoned to meet someone else who would be there.

Eventually, Sergeant started ordering people around and everyone jumped at his voice to do whatever he said. Steven was taken to a fine room and a servant was assigned to see that he ate, slept, ate, and dressed in time for the King's banquet the next night.

The bed was so soft that Steven scarcely slept all night. During the day, he was allowed to wander about the castle, always with the servant in tow, so he would not get lost. Of all the places in the castle he visited, Steven liked the kitchen the best. He tried not to get in the way, but commented on the seasonings and suggested herbs for the stew. Until he ate his noon meal, he was welcome to dabble with the kitchen help, but when the chief chef arrived to prepare the banquet for the evening, Steven was summarily shooed out as an army of kitchen help moved in to wash, chop, boil, sauté, roast, fry, and bake.

The servant assigned to Steven suggested they spend some time in the "game" room, which Steven assumed was a place where trophies of the hunt were kept. Or perhaps it was a zoo in which living species were on display from the King's Forest. Instead, he found a room in which the children of the castle gathered to play.

There were various toys, including balls for the children to play with. Some—made from the bladder of a pig, he was told—bounced off floors and walls, as laughing children threw them from one to the other. Other balls were smaller and harder and were used to throw at various targets. Steven was enthralled with the happiness of the children in the room and waded right in among them to play as well.

He was thrown a ball and threw it to another, hardly having it out of his hand before he had to catch a different ball. The children, happy to have a little boy who was as big as an adult playing with them, soon evolved a new game where every ball was passed to Steven as quickly as it was thrown back. Several of these, unfortunately, went uncaught. Steven did his best to dodge the balls as they came upon him at an ever-increasing speed.

The servant had taken refuge behind some stacked bales of straw, behind which were huddled a variety of nurses and servants who peeked out cautiously to watch the children.

Steven discovered there was a rhythm developing in the children's throws. Allowing one ball to hit him squarely in the chest and bounce off, he reached in the pocket of his vest and quickly put his whistle in his mouth. Although he couldn't play much of a tune with both hands involved in catching and throwing balls, he started to pipe the same rhythm that the sergeant had used to enforce his march through the forest. The children, easily influenced by the rhythm, matched it with their throws and were soon taking orderly turns, as Steven caught and threw balls with both hands. He began to step to the rhythm of the music in a pattern reminiscent of Selah's dance he had watched for the past seven years.

At one point, a nurse popped out from behind the straw to call the name of a child and usher her out of the room for "dressing." She threw her ball to Steve, and then vanished out the door with her nurse. Steven, not knowing what to do with the abandoned ball now that there was no one to throw it to, tossed it into the air while he caught and threw another, and then caught the ball again before it fell to the floor.

Apparently, it was time for the children to be bathed and dressed for dinner, for they were subsequently called by their nurses and servants, threw their balls to Steven, and rushed out of the room. Steven lost track of the number of balls in the air, but the rhythm he had established allowed him to keep many in the air and only a few fell to the floor.

At last, he was faced with just one child, whose nurse had taken another and just returned for this one. Steven looked at the child and the child looked at Steven. Steven threw the balls into the air and caught them automatically as he watched the child. The child threw the last ball to Steven.

All the balls fell to the floor as Steven reached to catch the last ball. The child laughed with glee as though this had been the best part of the day. He ran off with his nurse and there were no more children in the room.

Steven's servant appeared from behind the straw bales and called to him, as if he were one of the children. He led Steven away to be bathed and dressed for the banquet with the King.

MONTAGUE MAGNUS THE Fourth, King and Liege of Sylgale, Puissant Paragon of Mariria, and the Simple Pride of Arining, was a jovial monarch. Some said he was simple of mind. Others whispered that the King's simplicity was a front that allowed him to get the best of his enemies and to negotiate shrewdly. Certainly, the most recent victory over the King of the Southern Reaches in Byzantium seemed to be testament to this latter opinion.

Mariria, the city surrounding the castle, loved their King and enjoyed the stories of his misadventures. When Steven was led into the great hall where the banquet would take place, his presence was announced by a herald whose voice was considerably more authoritative than Sergeant's had been when delivering the message to Steven.

"My Liege, Princes and Princesses of the realm of Sylgale, Noble ladies and gentlemen of Arining, and people of Mariria! Tonight, for one night only, we are proud to present a man whose stories precede him; a man who has faced dangers unlike any we have known; a man who has mastered a dragon and faced down the legendary great brown bear of the King's Forest; who outwitted the famed thief of Baghalonia, and who has entertained in every town from here to Byzantium; who it is said knew the fabled road-builder Xandros and the legendary tinker Armand Hamar; and who has traveled in the company of the dragon-lady herself. In his first appearance at Castle Mariria, please welcome our most esteemed guest, Steven George the Dragonslayer, master of the Long Road, and teller of the world's story."

All the people in the crowded banquet hall stood and applauded. Not having actually recognized the description the herald had given as being his own introduction, Steven clapped his hands together as well, looking around to see the great celebrity who had been introduced. An escort of royal guards, led by none other than Sergeant himself, fell in on either side of Steven and escorted him to a spot next to the King.

Sergeant turned to Steven sharply and commanded, "Kneel."

Steven immediately fell to his knees before the King.

King Montague rose to his feet and offered a hand to Steven, raising him back to his feet. Then the King surprised the crowded room by embracing Steven and showing him to his chair. When the Monarch, too, had resumed his seat, the other patrons of the banquet sat as well. As soon as the King raised his fork, all the others raised their forks. The King paused long enough for Steven to get the message and lift his fork as well. Then the King stabbed a potato on his plate, and it disappeared beneath an enormous bushy gray mustache that bobbed up and down as the King chewed. Everyone in the hall fell to the food on their plates and began eating. Steven copied the King, and when the King put his fork down, so did Steven.

"Keep eating," said the King. "They only wait for me to take the first bite. It's part of the whole king-thing."

"Thank you, your er… Kingness," Steven said.

He tried to look into the King's eyes when he spoke, but they were all but hidden beneath busy eyebrows, nearly the size of the mustache. Steven hesitated, then continued to eat. He didn't taste the food or know precisely what he ate because he was so intent on paying attention to the King.

"The correct term is Your Majesty," the King instructed. "You could also say Your Highness if paying homage. Or if addressing me as the religious leader of the people, Your Grace. But come now, I didn't invite you all the way here to have your obeisance. When we are in private conversation, you may address me as Magnus. Montague is used only when referring to me or talking about me, as in, 'King Montague is an old fool,' which I am sure you will hear sometime if you haven't already. Magnus is the name I use in private. Of course, if addressing me in a way in which all these courtiers could hear you, you should continue to use Your Majesty."

"Yes, Your Majesty, er... Magnus," Steven stuttered. He was still overwhelmed by the experience of being in a castle, in the presence of a King, and in a crowd so large he could not count them. He watched in amazement as another whole potato on the King's plate was speared and disappeared beneath the bushy mustache.

"I have heard about your storytelling and want to experience it firsthand," said Magnus.

Steven nearly choked on the potato and began to push his chair back.

"I would be happy to tell you a story," Steven said. "Is there a particular one you would like to hear?"

"Sit, sit," said the King companionably. "I have studied the matter carefully. I am not here to tax you a story. I understand that stories are a means of commerce for you, and I intend to pay for that which I consume. And perhaps we shall both be a story richer for the trade. I shall tell my story first and then you will tell yours. Now, I will speak quietly to tell the story just to you, for it would not be fitting for the King to tell a story in the presence of the entire court."

The King dropped his voice and Steven leaned in to hear.

"If too many people heard the story I am about to tell you, they might begin to worry. And a kingdom that is worried is an unpleasant thing to rule. It would be vulnerable to enemies, if you take my drift. So, I have set this table for just the two of us, so that I may tell my tale openly to you. Then you may tell your story to the entire room, as you are a storyteller and the people gathered here have come to hear you tell a story. It was the only way I could get the room full."

Steven nodded and sat to listen to the King's story.

7
The Thief of Kings

ONCE UPON A TIME, at the birth of the nations, there was a man who would be King. It might surprise you to know that there was nothing special about him. He wasn't born a king, nor was he of royal lineage. In fact, there was nothing about him that would distinguish him from anyone else you might have met at that time. He was completely ordinary.

His one defining characteristic was his fierce love of land. Not "the" land as in a particular country. Just land. He loved land. In fact, the area where he lived was much too crowded for him, so he packed up his meager possessions and moved away.

Far away.

He walked past the last farmhouse and continued on until he met no more people. When he had met no people while traveling for three days, he walked on another three days, just to be sure. At last, he began to look for a place to live. The place had to be rich in wild game and fertile soil. It had to have ready materials for building his shelter. It had to be high where he could see the terrain and defend it if that became necessary. You see, in all these things, he thought like a king.

Finally, he came to a high hill, clear on the side that

faced out looking over a vast sea, and bordered on the other by a dense forest. All around him he saw fertile fields and plentiful game. There was wood and stone to build with and he was pleased. As he stood at the top of that hill, he looked all around him and shouted out at the top of his lungs, "I claim this land as my own! I am King of All I survey!" He took an axe and cut a tall sapling, stripping it and driving it into the ground at the center of the hill. To the sapling he tied an old shirt and proudly declared it the Kingdom of Allisurvey. Then he set to work.

One thing you must say for this young king was that he was industrious. In one summer, he built a strong shelter atop the hill, he planted crops, he set traps and fishing lines. He was certain it would be a long cold winter and was determined to be ready for it.

The winter came and he was snug in his house with plenty of food and a warm fire. He busied himself with tasks that could be done in the cold weather, like tanning skins and sewing clothing. And in the spring, he began again to plant and hunt and fish and build. It was not long before he had shelter enough for a family and perhaps even a friend. So, he decided to return to the town he had come from and entice a bride and perhaps a friend to return to his kingdom.

But before he left, he decided to fully survey the Kingdom of Allisurvey. He walked the perimeter of his lands as far away as he could get and still see the shirt flag that now flew from a pole atop his house. At this point he drove a stake into the ground and hung a small scrap of hide. And so he went, all the way around his land.

When he was satisfied, he reckoned that he had time for a journey to and from his former home to collect his bride and friend.

It was not a difficult journey, but it was difficult convincing anyone to join him in his new kingdom. And this was when he showed his true colors. Unable to woo a bride, he determined to steal one. He traded for the few supplies he felt he would need, and in the middle of the night, in the middle of the town square, the King of Allisurvey declared war on the town.

He stole into a home where he had seen a woman he desired enter, tied her up in her sleep, emptied her wardrobe and larder, loaded all he could carry into his cart, and left town. As he left the town behind, he turned to look back at it and announced, "I accept your surrender."

Now you might think that a stolen bride is as good as no bride at all, but the thief King kept her bound to the wagon until he reached his homestead, by which time the poor girl was so lost, she dared not run away. He became progressively more kind to her and if she did not grow to love him, she grew to accept her fate and tolerate him.

Though it sounds strange to us in this age—barbaric— it was not an uncommon practice in that far distant past. May it never come upon us again!

Now, the work of two people on the land caused it to be even more productive, and before long there was a son in the house as well. Each year at the end of harvest, King Alli, as he called himself, would walk the perimeter of his kingdom, and move the survey stakes outward away from the flag ten paces.

One summer, a traveler approached the little kingdom and the King of Allisurvey went out to meet him, and offer him hospitality or a challenge, as seemed appropriate. It happened that the man was searching for just such a land as King Alli possessed. He saw Alli's wife and how productive his land was, and he determined to possess it.

But concealing his desires, he enjoyed the hospitality of the royal table and slept near the hearth.

Alli's wife was both smart and ruthless—learning well from her husband. Weighing the possibilities of being a slave to one man or the other, she chose the evil she knew over the one she did not. She warned Alli that the traveler was not sleeping. When the traveler came to kill Alli and take his wife, she helped Alli throw a net over the intruder and subdue him. The visitor became a prisoner.

Alli gave the traveler a simple choice. He could remain, bound to a rock and in servitude to the royals, or he could be slain with his own sword. The traveler chose the former and entered into servitude to King Alli.

With an additional pair of hands—even bound to the rock that he had to carry with him everywhere—the Kingdom of Allisurvey prospered. Prospered in that there was plentiful food and shelter for all its residents. And each fall, Alli moved the stakes of his kingdom out another ten paces.

Realizing that he could no longer survey all his land from the hill top, he built his house taller and raised his flag higher.

I SHAN'T SPEAK of all the ways that King Alli and his sons, and even, eventually, his servant, recruited more people to their distant kingdom. Suffice it to say that the little kingdom often declared war on the outskirts of another land and then accepted surrender, whether given or not, as they carried away more people and wealth. These foreign lands seldom knew they had been at war and lost.

And every year, Alli and his wife and his children would walk the perimeter of the kingdom and move the border stakes out ten paces—never more, never less. Every year, they built the homestead larger and taller, so the tattered flag could be seen from farther away.

When King Alli was very old, he built a great tower where he spent the remainder of his days looking out at Allisurvey.

Though King Alli founded a country, it was not so large as it is today; for each year, the spirit of King Alli is said to go to the borders and move the stakes ten paces farther out. So, the kingdom has grown to this day, stealing a bit from other kingdoms each year.

Some say the spirit has turned malevolent. Others say it has always been Alli himself who declares war on villages and carries away women for his harem. But the reigning King of Allisurvey, which is known today as Arining, knows that a new and darker force than the Thief of Kings is plundering his borders.

King Alli was always expanding the territory, but for these seven years, the marker posts have moved closer in. Now, it is the women of the villages of Arining who are carried away. Some new pretender is about, attempting to steal the kingdom and terrorize the people.

So, the King, today, has sent for a great Master of Dragons, to send him into the farthest reaches of the kingdom, there to master the Terror of Rich Reach, the wealthiest and most remote province of the country; for surely if he has mastered his dragon, he can master his terror as well.

8
Banquet

STEVEN SAT STARING at the King, who fell to eating his bowl of soup with vigor, splashing a good bit into his bushy mustache.

It suddenly dawned on him that he was not here to simply tell stories with the King. He was here because the King expected him to go to this Rich Reach—wherever that was—and master whoever or whatever was terrorizing it. Whatever was terrorizing Rich Reach was also now terrorizing Steven.

"Your Majesty!" Steven exclaimed. "You can't mean to say that you want me to go hunt an unknown terror! I've not actually slain a dragon. I'm really just a storyteller. I have no skills in knowing what the terror is that you seek. I can't…"

Steven stuttered to a pause, too overwhelmed to speak.

"Relax," said the King. "It's just a story. You don't expect everyone to believe there was really an ogre threatening a village that was overcome by a ridiculous hat, do you? Or that a miser gave up his hoard of gold to a thief in exchange for a cup? They are just stories."

"How do you know the stories that I have told?" asked Steven.

"Oh, stories travel much faster than people," Magnus replied, laughing. "Let's see. There was a war a few years ago. Now, unlike bridges, wars are a great boon to commerce. There were certain knights captured who had come across a dragonslayer who told magnificent stories. They, in turn, traded the stories for a better place in the prisons. A merchant came to negotiate the truce and he told of a dragonslayer who told stories. He traded a story for the release of our prisoners of war. Ah… Then there was the thief."

Just at that point, servants interrupted to clear the soup bowls and a procession of cooks with silver platters began from the kitchen to the tables. The chief cook approached the King's table himself, and with a flourish, removed the cover of his tray.

"Duck!" the King exclaimed.

Steven dove under the table.

Seeing Steven dive for cover, Magnus dove under the table as well. When the King disappeared beneath the head table, there was a shocked silence, then every guest in the hall took cover beneath the banquet tables. There was a loud clatter as silver trays hit the floor and cooks crammed themselves under the closest tables. Sergeant and all the King's guards rushed to surround the King's table with swords drawn to defend their liege. At last, the room was silent as the guards surveyed the surround area with their eyes.

Under the table the King uncovered his head to look at Steven who cowered there, shaking. Steven slowly looked up into the King's eyes. As one, they spoke.

"Is it safe?"

They crept from beneath the cover of the table.

"Sergeant!" barked the King. "Is it safe?"

"We see nothing up here that might make it unsafe, Your Majesty," Sergeant replied. Cautiously, the King and

Steven regained their seats. The guests crawled from beneath the tables and worriedly sat in their chairs. The cooks quickly scraped the food back onto their trays, placed them on the tables, and fled to the kitchen. Sergeant leaned in toward the King's table, still not taking his eyes of the surrounds.

"What was it?" whispered the King to Steven.

"I don't know," answered Steven.

"Was it a shadow?" asked Sergeant. "A premonition? A sudden movement?"

Everyone looked at Steven.

"You said, 'Duck!' Your Majesty."

The King looked at Sergeant, then at the silver tray before them, the lid still partially covering it. Busker lifted the lid cautiously with his sword pointing at it.

"It's a duck," whispered Magnus.

"Oh," said Steven. "I thought it was the Terror."

"Ha!" laughed Sergeant. "Now that will make a story even I would listen to!"

The guards returned to their posts, and as the story spread through the great hall, nervous laughter rippled in its wake. As everyone tore into the only slightly soiled fowls on their tables, the mood began to relax throughout the hall and the laughter became louder and almost hysterical.

"Do you see what this Terror has done to my Kingdom?" asked Magnus. "That is why we don't speak of it aloud. Even though the attacks have occurred leagues away from the city, everyone is nervous. Even me."

"I was going to take the southern route along the sea," Steven said forlornly. "I didn't intend to come here at all."

"No one *intends* to come here," the King replied. "Eat your… quacker, before you tell us a story. Perhaps you can point the way to how we can master our Terror."

"When I have told my story," said Steven, "may I return to the South Road along the sea?"

"Yes, of course," said the King. "But I don't think you will want to."

"Why is that?" asked Steven. He had already mastered a dragon and been faced by the bear. He could not see what else could lie along the South Road that would be more dangerous than continuing to Rich Reach to face the Terror.

"Well now, that would be another story," said the King, "but the gist of it is this. In Rich Reach, there awaits a reward for the person who masters the Terror. I know that you are not tempted by rewards or I would have offered gold. But you may wish to reclaim certain property that stories say was taken from you years ago. Prince Montague Valentine of Rich Reach has promised a sword and dagger—each etched with the figure of a dragon so fiery it glows from the steel—to the man or woman who masters the Terror of Rich Reach."

Steven let his mouth fall open at the words. He had once trusted a thief named Pablo Bárcenas Ibin Ariaga. In the morning, he had awakened in a stable. His horse, his coins, his sword, and the dagger that Armand Hamar the Tinker had etched for him were all gone. In their place was a donkey. The humiliation Steven felt when the guards escorted him to the city gates, gave him three silver coins, and told him never to return to Byzantium, still stung The Dragonslayer's eyes.

"How did the Prince come to have this sword and dagger?" asked Steven.

"Let us just say that a certain thief was captured and his property confiscated," said the King. "That is a story you may find along the road to Rich Reach, but it is not one I am inclined to share."

Steven finished his dinner in silence with the excuse of thinking about the story he was about to tell. Understanding the temperament of "the artist," the King excused the silence. He confessed that he, too, often brooded in silence before a particularly difficult public address. In the meantime, the King and all his subjects helped themselves to more wine and were in a riotously good mood when Steven finally rose to tell his story.

9
The Bottomless Pocket

ONCE UPON A TIME, in an age of tiny miracles, a wood elf named Panjameon was out walking in his woodland, playing merrily on a pipe and dancing in time to the music he played. As he walked, he became hungry. Seeing a bee flit into a hole in a tree trunk, Panjameon thought he might find honey to satisfy his appetite. He approached the tree cautiously, not wanting to be stung, but he saw no further sign of bees. He listened at the hole for the longest time, but heard no telltale buzzing, and saw no bees come out of the hole.

At last, he looked into the hole, but it was dark inside and he could see no sign of a beehive or a bee. This puzzled Panjameon, so he carefully and slowly reached his hand into the hole to feel around for honeycomb. He felt no honeycomb. In fact, what he felt was remarkably soft, like the fur of an animal. Panjameon withdrew his hand and walked around the tree to the other side, but there was no hole on the other side of the tree.

Next, Panjameon made a small torch out of bark and grasses and thrust the torch into the tree. But the torch did nothing to reveal the inside of the hole, and as Panjameon extended his hand farther and farther into the tree, the torch seemed to disappear in the darkness. Panjameon

52

could not feel the other side of the hole that seemed to go on forever.

Again, Panjameon walked around the tree. He stretched out his arm and measured it against the width of the tree. His arm was much longer than the breadth of the tree.

This small miracle might have been enough for most people to discover and walk away shaking their heads in wonder, but Panjameon wanted to know more about the mysterious hole that seemed to have no bottom. So, after much thought and hesitation, Panjameon stuck his head in the hole. Darkness met his eyes and he thrust the torch into the hole with his head. This did little to illuminate his surroundings, but Panjameon discovered that he could get both arms into the hole with his head and soon he was up to his waist in the tree.

That was when Panjameon saw it—light. It seemed a bit far off at first, but as he wiggled farther into the tree, the light seemed much closer. At last, his feet left the ground, he pressed his whole body up and into the tree, and his head popped out the other side.

The 'other side' as Panjameon thought of it, was not a tree. Instead, he found himself looking out of the pocket of a sheepskin jacket, bouncing merrily along as a farm boy walked jauntily into a village. Panjameon shrank back in fear because he had obviously entered a land of giants.

"This giant's pocket contains my entire world!" exclaimed Panjameon. After his moment of fear, Panjameon's curiosity got the best of him and he pushed his head out of the pocket again.

The boy had stopped where a pancake seller had set up his shop and was negotiating the price of breakfast. Panjameon realized just in time that the boy's hand was reaching for the pocket. He dove down into the depths of the pocket and scrambled around over mounds of loose miscellaneous and mostly unidentified objects. Panjameon looked up and saw the little light blocked out as the hand reached down into the pocket.

"Coins," thought Panjameon. "He must be reaching for a coin to buy his breakfast."

As the hand stretched toward him in the pocket, Panjameon scrambled among the piles at the bottom, found a coin, and thrust it up where the descending fingers could feel it. The coin was almost as big as Panjameon, and when the fingers touched it, they lifted it out of the pocket so rapidly that Panjameon scarcely had time to let go before being dragged out into the open. The boy exchanged coin for pancake and happily resumed his stroll.

Panjameon returned to the opening of the pocket and watched as the boy was joined by two others, and the three followed a village girl, while laughing and giggling. The boy moved closer rapidly while reaching for the pocket. Panjameon dove into the pocket again and as the hand descended, pushed the first thing he came in contact with into the grasping fingers.

He heard the girl scream as the frog the boy had grabbed slid down her back.

Not long after, the boy and his friends played in the woods making a lean-to. One of the boys said they needed to tie the frame together and once again the boy's hand reached to his pocket. Knowing what he was looking for this time, Panjameon thrust a piece of hemp twine into the boy's hand.

Panjameon began to enjoy the game and explored the depths of the pocket, which seemed to have no end. Every time he saw the hand descend from the opening of the pocket, he would push something else into it—an apple for eating, a flat stone for skipping, flint for making a fire, a whistle for playing a tune. Panjameon didn't even need to think about what the boy wanted; he just pushed the next thing at hand into the boy's fingers.

When the boy slept at night, Panjameon searched through the giant's house and village for things that might come in handy for the boy. Each item he stuffed into the boy's pocket. No matter how much Panjameon put into the pocket, there was always room for more. And Panjameon, too.

Panjameon so enjoyed the bottomless pocket that he began to travel farther away, both in his own world and in the boy giant's. He gathered new things to stuff in the pocket. No matter what the boy's need, Panjameon always had something to put in his hand from the miraculous pocket.

And so, the boy grew older and became a giant of a man. The vest that had once been so large on him, now fit snugly. But still the young giant always found just what he needed in his pocket.

Eventually, as often happens to young men, Panjameon's giant fell in love. Panjameon recognized the object of his affection as the same girl giant who received a frog down her back on Panjameon's first day with the giant.

The girl was coy, but pleased with the giant's attention. As the couple walked through the market one day, the girl's dress caught on the corner of a stall and tore. Quick as a wink, Panjameon's giant drew a needle and thread from his pocket and sewed up the dress. Then a wind came up and the young woman's hair began to blow in her face. The giant reached in his pocket and pulled out a ribbon to tie back her locks.

When the couple reached the door of the girl's home, they discovered it locked. The giant reached in his pocket and brought forth a key that let them in. The girl thought to cook a meal for the two of them, but in the process dropped an egg on the floor. The giant reached in his pocket and produced another egg that she fried while he cleaned up the broken mess on the floor with a brush he pulled from his pocket.

After they had dined, the giant proposed that the girl come to live with him as his mate. She wept and he reached in his pocket for a napkin with which to dry her tears. When she said yes, the giant pulled a ring from his pocket and placed it on her hand. It seemed that no matter what the young man needed, all he had to do was reach into his pocket and the answer was at hand.

I will not try to describe all the impossible things that the giant pulled from his pocket over the years, looked over by Panjameon the wood elf, who thought it great fun to keep the bottomless pocket stocked with whatever might be needed in the future.

As things would have it, generations passed. The vest and its bottomless pocket passed from one to the next. It is that remarkable garment that I wear myself today.

Now, you might ask if I found my own way to the land of giants to steal the vest, but I tell you, no. This land where we live is the land of giants that Panjameon once feared and grew to love. For being a giant is a matter of perspective. Like all else I have ever needed, the tiny wood elf may still dwell in the pocket of my vest.

10
Beginning

S TEVEN BREAKFASTED with the King. The banquet and the storytelling had gone well, in spite of the small disruption at the arrival of the main course. Many people had approached Steven respectfully at the end of the banquet to touch the magical sheepskin vest that he wore. While no one dared reach into his pocket, Steven was aware that a young woman who smiled at him also dropped a key in his pocket; an aspiring courtier hoping to gain favor at court dropped a coin in the pocket; and a particularly handsome duke sniffed slightly and dropped a small mirror in Steven's pocket. Steven, himself, was a little surprised that his pocket did not bulge out.

Steven had spent a restless night, working out his decision regarding which road he would take in the morning. He had a strong desire to flee from the Kingdom and return to the southbound road where he had left Madame Selah Welinska. But the thought that the knife Armand Hamar had engraved for him and the sword that he had acquired in Byzantium might be waiting for him in Rich Reach was tantalizing beyond belief. Ultimately, Steven had decided that he would go the way of the King's Road, deeper into the Kingdom of Arining. After all, he reminded himself, all roads lead to his dragon.

And thus, after breakfast, Steven shouldered his pack, his bow, and his staff, and set his face toward the city gates. The King embraced Steven again and gave Steven a small flag that, upon closer examination, looked remarkably like a shirt for a very small person.

"This will identify you to any who ask as an emissary of the King," he said. Steven slipped the flag into his pocket. The King noticed and lowered his voice. "I must ask," said the King, "is it true that everything you need is in your pocket?"

"The truth is," Steven said, "that I have never needed much."

"Ah," said the King. "Good travels, Steven George the Dragonslayer."

"Thank you, Your Majesty," Steven replied formally; and then he began his journey out of the palace and toward the city gates.

Many people had gathered to watch Steven's departure and to cheer him on as their champion to face the Terror. The first to meet Steven, however, was Sergeant.

"Will you be traveling with me, Sergeant?" Steven asked.

"No, my duty is here with the King," Sergeant answered. "But I have a gift for you that may do you some good." With that, Sergeant presented Steven with a loop of twine, to which a small stone was tied. Steven hefted the tiny rock. It was too small to be used as a weapon. It was not pretty enough to be worn as jewelry. He puzzled over it.

"From the very beginning," Sergeant said, "the members of the King's guard have worn a rock in memory of our ancestor who served the King while bound to a rock. This marks you, Steven George, as a recruit in the King's

Guard." Sergeant paused then added in a low voice, "For protecting the King from a deadly waterfowl."

Steven and Sergeant both laughed at this, and after Sergeant slapped Steven on the back, the Dragonslayer placed the rock lanyard in his pocket and continued toward the city gates. He had not gone far, however, when the King's cook rushed from the palace to catch up with him.

"We met only briefly when I shooed you from my kitchen and then again under a tablecloth," said the cook, "but I could not let you leave to face the Terror without some lunch." The cook handed Steven an oilskin packet. "It's a duck sandwich," the cook whispered. Then he scurried off to return to his kitchen.

Steven smiled at the joke and placed the sandwich in his pocket. Just before he reached the gate of the city, however, a flock of children blocked his way. The children were silent, but pushed one of the smallest forward. The shy child looked up at Steven and smiled, then threw a ball to him. This was quickly followed by two more balls that Steven began to juggle.

The children shrieked with laughter and danced around Steven as he left through the city gate on the road to Rich Reach, juggling the brightly colored balls as he walked. He was now fifty-nine thousand three hundred seventy-one steps from where he had left Selah and was bound for a new adventure. Just outside the city gates, a large wooden post showed a carving of a sword and dagger, pointing ahead along the road to Rich Reach.

"Just follow the signs," yelled Sergeant from the parapet at the gate. "It's the mark of Rich Reach." Steven lengthened his stride and was soon out of sight of all but the flag at the topmost tower of the castle.

THE ROAD HE walked the first day was broad and well-traveled, with villages at the side of the road every few thousand steps. Wherever he went, people called him by name and waved. A feeling of gloom in the villages seemed to lift a little as he passed through. When at last he came to the end of the day, he was invited to stay at the home of a weaver and his wife, the spinner, at the edge of a tiny village. Outside the handsome cottage was an open-sided shed that was piled full of shearling wool.

"Welcome to the home of Zurbaran the Weaver and Orithyia the Spinner," said the slender man at the door of the cottage. "We would be pleased if you joined us for dinner and took respite here for the night before your journey into the darkness."

The man made Steven's quest sound dire, and acted as if Steven were being offered the last meal of a condemned prisoner.

"Zurbie, have a heart!" exclaimed a round little woman with flaming rosy cheeks and a mouth that seemed permanently bent into a jovial smile. "The poor boy is on a grand adventure and you make it sound like he's marching to his death. Come in here, dearie, and let's have dinner." The woman's presence was all the light the small cottage needed, but the cheerful fire and hot food were equally welcome. The weaver scarcely said a word during the meal, but his wife chatted non-stop.

"I'm a bit of a storyteller myself," she said proudly.

"Really?" asked Steven, thinking a good Once Upon a Time might be just the thing to further brighten the evening.

"Oh yes," she said. "I'm always spinning yarns!" She laughed at her joke and the weaver rolled his eyes heavenward. "Of course, Zurbie weaves a fine tale as well," she continued to laugh. "Now where was I?" she asked. "I seem to have lost my thread of thought!" Her laughter and humor were contagious to Steven and he joined the laughter. The weaver adopted the demeanor of a long-suffering husband who had heard it all before.

"It must be the wine," laughed Steven. "My head's a little woolly." Orithyia howled with more laughter as Zurbaran poured himself more wine.

"'Twill be a long night if we keep this up," laughed Orithyia.

Steven choked and held his throat as his eyes suddenly bulged. Alarmed, Zurbaran jumped to slap him on the back. After a short span of coughing, Steven gulped some more wine. "It's all right," he gasped. "I just got a herringbone caught in my throat!"

Orithyia burst out laughing again.

"All right!" shouted the weaver, jumping up from his seat. "I'll tell a story. Just no more, please!"

11
The Shrouded Muse

ONCE UPON A TIME, behind the ivory veil that separates our world from that of spirits and demons, there lived a proud prince named Walrath the Fierce. He was given his name because in battle there was none so brave as Walrath.

At the battle of Moritia, Walrath slew a thousand enemies in a fight that lasted from the rising of the sun to its setting on the following day. When no enemies came forth to do battle, Walrath sought them out in their hiding places. It is said that Walrath would make enemies just for the joy of slaying them.

But Walrath had a secret desire. He had kept it hidden in his heart for so long that it scarcely flickered in his eyes. But it remained a pain deep inside. When he was not out killing his enemies, Walrath sat alone in his high-walled castle brooding.

Walrath's mother, the Queen, had long known that Walrath had a secret desire, though he had never spoken of it. She saw, as only a mother can, that something was amiss in her son from the very earliest age. When he was but a baby, he would have fits of rage and flail his fists. It was only his mother's voice crooning lullabies to him that could soothe his soul.

Music seemed such a soothing influence on her son that the queen ordered musicians in the castle to play at all hours of the day and night. But when war threatened, the musicians were dismissed and Walrath marched into battle fiercer than before.

It was at the end of the war with Rocklaven that Walrath was changed. There was scarcely a soldier left alive in the Rocklaven monarch's army, and wandering in the hills searching for those who fled, Walrath heard a voice. He caught just a bit of the tune and the melodic voice, and then it faded away. It was just enough for Walrath to want more. He wandered for days through the mountains and hills, catching a bit of music from "just over there" or a melody from "just beyond." Each time he heard the music, his heart was filled with greater desire, and so he followed.

When Walrath had wandered for a full cycle of the moon, chasing after the mysterious musical voice, he found that he was deep in a strange and unknown territory. But the voice was less fleeting now and seemed much nearer, so he forged ahead. At last, he came to the mouth of a cave from which the music issued continuously. He found that he needed more courage to enter this cave than he had needed to face entire armies on the battlefield. But somehow, he found that courage from the desire buried in his heart, and he entered into the gloom of the cave.

There he found a shrouded figure playing a lute and singing in the sweetest voice Walrath had ever heard. He lay down his sword and sat before the figure, enrapt with the music she played. When at last she spoke to him, it was in dulcet tones that scarcely differed from her singing.

"What is it that you desire, Walrath the Fierce?" she asked melodically.

Now, in any court or before any king, Walrath would have shouted, "Victory!" But the smooth tones of the shrouded woman brooked no lies and Walrath searched deep in his heart for the hidden desire.

"Music," he said in a hoarse whisper. "I have always wanted to make music."

The shrouded woman's laughter fell like a gentle rain on Walrath's ready ears. He felt he had never heard such a beautiful sound in his life.

"Why then, why don't you?" asked the woman.

"I dare not," answered Walrath. "It would make me weak. My warriors would not follow me."

"So, you want to make music without anyone knowing it is you making music," mused the lady. "But there is no secret music only you can hear. The delight of making music is having others listen to it."

"You make music in secret," responded Walrath.

"I am secret, but not my music," answered the muse. "Perhaps that is the answer to your problem."

The lady rose from her seat and approached Walrath, who watched in silence and peace. Whatever she did, he was content to let it happen. He marveled that he could ever know such peace in his heart.

A slender hand reached from beneath the shroud holding the singer's lute.

"Take it," she said. Walrath accepted the lute. "Hold it as tenderly as your lover. Caress its strings gently. If you would have it give you music, you must coax it out with kindness and love."

Walrath hesitantly stroked the strings. The sound was harsh and he changed his grip as she spoke in her musical voice. He coaxed the lute with his fingertips and asked it as a supplicant to give him music. And, indeed, it did. The clear tone was followed by a change in Walrath. He lifted his face to the lady and a smile warmed his expression. The lady leaned over him. He felt her lips pressed against his through the thin fabric of the shroud. Then the fabric began to fall over him. It draped his figure as he sat on the ground in the cave. It darkened all that was around him.

"Now you are secret," whispered the voice of the muse from all around him. "As long as you wear the veil, no one will know that it is you who plays the lute. No one will know it is your voice that sings the ballads. But there is one limitation that you must know. As long as you live, you will never be able to slay a musician—not in battle, or anger, or passion. Beware and know that is your true weakness."

"I could never slay a musician anyway," laughed Walrath.

He was ecstatic that he had found the answer to his heart's desire beneath the shroud. But he was curious as well.

"I should like to know my benefactor," he said pulling the shroud from around his head. But there in the cave, was only darkness. He found no one there.

Walrath wandered back through the mountains and hills with the shroud over him, learning the contours and tone of the lute and discovering how it responded to him as if he were learning the body of a lover. Occasionally, he happened upon some shepherd or farmer who paused to stare agape at the shrouded figure that passed playing heavenly music.

But when Walrath was within sight of the walls of his castle, he removed the shroud and wrapped the lute in it. Thus, he returned to his guise as Prince Walrath the Fierce.

When he entered the gates of the castle, his soldiers and servants bowed before him and rushed to do his bidding. The castle lived in fear of its master.

Walrath rushed to his chamber and carefully hid the lute and shroud. After bathing and refreshing his appearance, he emerged on the ramparts of the castle to review his troops. He had been gone and considered lost for more than two cycles of the moon, but everything seemed to be in order when he had finished his inspection.

Late that night, a shrouded figure made its first appearance on the castle walls. The music reached the soldiers below and they set out to capture the intruder. Realizing his mistake, Walrath fled, pulling the shroud from his head and wrapping it around his lute.

The next day, Prince Walrath issued a decree forbidding anyone to approach or hinder the passage of the shrouded singer. His soldiers were surprised, but when the figure appeared on the parapets again that night and the next, they made no move to hinder him. Many found themselves strangely at peace for the first time in their lives.

It was, therefore, with disappointed shock that they found Wolflok, Warlord of the Steppes had invaded the principality. Prince Walrath ordered his troops to prepare to move out. The two armies faced each other across a great field where the battle would take place. The camps were both in unrest. Men found it hard to sleep before marching to battle. Then, the shrouded musician appeared. He walked the entire length of the field playing and singing and bringing peaceful sleep to all who heard him.

In the morning, when Walrath's army rose to do battle, they found Wolflok and his horde had left the field and returned home. A few days later, an emissary appeared at the gates of the castle escorting a beautiful princess, the sister of Wolflok.

"Wolflok, Warlord of the Steppes, sends greetings to the most feared Prince Walrath the Fierce and sues for peace between our nations," intoned the emissary. "In token of honor for our pledge, we present to Walrath our sister, Princess Ursula, to consider for his marriage. May union between our royal houses make long the peace between our nations."

Now, Walrath had no mind to marry, but when he saw the beautiful princess and she told him how happy she was to be considered as his bride, he thought himself a fortunate man indeed. If there was no war on the borders of his land, there would be no need for him to don his armor and leave behind the shroud of desire that he wore each night. This seemed good to Walrath and so he consented to marry the princess, with thoughts of living happily ever after.

The princess was, in fact, very willing to please Walrath, and he found his choice to be pleasurable without measure. However, late in the night, he would still rise and drape the shroud over himself to wander the ramparts and the city, playing the lute and singing.

Over the course of a year, Walrath became very comfortable with his very enthusiastic wife. The country was at peace, and Walrath got to play music every night. But Princess Ursula was clever, and it was not long before she associated the nightly music of the shrouded figure with her husband leaving the room.

She carefully probed about the singer, but Walrath was always on his guard and did not tell her anything she could use. When he grew tired of her questions, he would say, "The singer is a phantom that soothes my kingdom," or "The shrouded singer is the spirit of all those I have killed in battle, and I must attend to it each night or have nightmares." Each time she asked, he made up a different story, but never told her the truth.

When they had been married a year and a day, Walrath entered the royal chamber to find his wife packing her bags.

"What is the meaning of this?" Walrath asked in disbelief.

"Truly husband, you do not love me," said Princess Ursula, "so I have decided to return to my homeland."

"But I do love you," said the Prince. "More than life itself." And as he spoke the words, he realized they were true, for his wife had won him body and soul.

"You do not love me," said Princess Ursula. "Otherwise, why would you always lie to me about the shrouded singer and desert my bed in the middle of the night? If you really loved me, you would tell me the truth."

Now Walrath was sorely vexed. He loved his wife, but the muse had told him explicitly not to let anyone know the secret of the shroud. But, he reasoned, a husband and wife are truly one person. There is no difference between the two and should be no barriers between them. And having reasoned thus, Walrath sat with Ursula and told her all that had befallen him in the mountains.

"Now, truly, I know you love me!" exclaimed his wife. She swept the bags from the royal bed and drew him to her. Walrath slept in his wife's arms that night and the mysterious shrouded singer did not appear on the castle's walls.

When Walrath awoke in the morning, he felt refreshed and alive as he had never been before. He felt as though he was a free man; that his spirit had transcended the mortal and was bound to a new height.

Then he found that the Princess was not in bed with him. He searched through the chamber, but she was not there. He went to the kitchens and the gardens, to the stables and the kennels, but the Princess was not there.

Princess Ursula had, in fact, left in the middle of the night when Walrath slept and the castle guards waited for the shrouded singer to appear.

What was worse, she had stolen the shroud and lute from Walrath's hiding place.

Walrath despaired. He retired to his chamber and refused to emerge. With the shrouded singer missing from the ramparts of the castle, the soldiers and villagers alike began to worry and to bicker among themselves. As the Prince continued to build his rage alone in his chamber, fights broke out on the streets and in the barracks. Even though there was no war, there was also no peace. When Prince Walrath the Fierce emerged from his chamber, he was angrier and more vengeful than he had ever been before. He rallied his troops and rode at their head toward the Steppes, there to do battle with Wolflok, to regain his princess.

Wolflok was already there and waiting. They came to face each other at the same field where the mysterious shrouded musician had played over a year before.

The camps were restless. No sleep came to them and the shrouded singer did not appear between the camps to lull them to sleep. When morning came, Walrath strode onto the field of battle with his banner raised high and his sword drawn. But as the armies closed to do battle, Walrath heard something new. Wolflok's entire army was whistling a marching tune as they came to meet Walrath's army. Walrath found his sword arm paralyzed. He faced soldiers coming toward him with swords drawn, but could not fight them because they whistled a tune. They were musicians, and they cut through Walrath's army clean as a whistle.

Before the Prince fell, he knew for a fact that his wife had betrayed him, for he saw at the top of a hill behind the opposing army, the shrouded figure of a singer, silhouetted against the darkening sky.

It is said that the shrouded muse still roams the hills of that kingdom, and that those who hear her music, hear also the screams of the dying Prince.

CHILLS RAN DOWN Steven's spine as he stared at the weaver. For the first time since he met him, the weaver smiled at Steven.

"Your turn," Zurbaran said, folding his arms.

Steven swallowed more wine and then began his story.

The Disenchanted Evening

ONCE UPON A TIME, there was a maiden who sat by her well sighing. Monette, which was her name, had followed all the advice of the village wise woman. She had bathed in the running waters of a stream. It was so cold that she thought she would never be able to get out of the water once she got in, but she did what she was told. She dressed in a linen gown that had never been worn before. She tied sprigs of pink lilacs in her hair with a blue ribbon. She had gathered daisies from the hillsides and dropped them one at a time into the well, and now, she sat sadly and waited.

She sighed again. All she wanted was a husband, and not that crude sheep farmer down the road. She wanted a handsome husband who was wealthy and lived in a beautiful house in the city. She wanted him to ride up to her on a white charger with the sun glinting from his armor. She wanted him to sweep her up into his arms and carry her away from the dull, dreary life she led in the tiny village where her destiny was naught but to cook, tend a home, and raise her children. She didn't want much.

That was what she thought of domestic life. In her eyes, the women of the village were old fools who never dreamed. They married their neighbors, bore their children, and cooked, cleaned, wove, and sewed their precious lives away. There must, she thought, be a higher purpose in life.

Whenever she thought of the sheep farmer who lived near her home and who had come to court her just that morning, her flesh crawled. Oh, he was polite and had never given her cause to be offended. He bathed before he came to call, so there was no smell of sheep about him. But he was so… common. He was a gangling youth whom she had known since birth. His shocking red hair stuck up from his head in so many directions that it appeared his head was on fire. And freckles. One could hardly tell if the red splotches or the white splotches were his actual skin color, for it was divided equally between the two. His trousers were too big for him, and when tying twine around his waist failed to keep them up properly, he tied the cord over his shoulder, suspending them like a sack held open and his long legs unceremoniously dumped into them.

But worst of all was the sheepskin. It was one thing to wear the sheep's rough wool woven into cloth and sewed together. It was quite another to wear the sheep's skin, cut in pieces and sewed together. And the farmer did just that. He wore boots made from sheepskin. He wore a hat made from sheepskin. He wore mittens made from sheepskin. And he wore a sheepskin vest so big that from a distance, one might mistake the boy for an oversized member of his own flock.

He was courteous enough when he came to call, and was totally undeserving of the rough rebuke she gave him when he asked for her hand.

"Soren Markladen," she said to him, "I cannot imagine a life in which I marry a freckle-faced sheep, eat mutton for every meal, wear woolskins for clothing, and raise a flock of little sheep for children. I cannot marry you. I will not marry you. Go back to your sheep and do not try to woo me further."

Soren Markladen, you might think, would be highly offended by the vain girl's rebuke, but in truth, he had grown to love her over the years they had known each other. They had often had adventures with each other and when she'd had difficulty with a fox snatching her hens, Soren had hunted the fox and presented the skin to her as a token of his devotion. She thought the fox skin was disgusting.

He willingly overlooked what others saw as her flaws. Most of these had to do with her temperament, but by the standards of his village, she was considered too short, too thin in some places and too thick in others, pale in complexion, and frail in physique. He, however, saw her as petite, pleasingly proportioned, fair, and delicate. Her temper he was willing to overlook.

So, instead of being upset by Monette's rejection, Soren was amused, nodded, and said, "My, she is spirited." He resolved to come and press his suit again the next day.

That was when Monette went to see the wise woman. She asked for the old woman's advice. She said she wanted to attract a handsome, rich, and caring husband who would carry her away from her life of drudgery and show her the excitement of life in the city. The old woman laughed to herself, and prescribed the ritual that Monette had just completed.

She sighed again.

"What is it that makes you sigh as though the world were ending?" a voice near her ear asked quietly.

Monette was surprised by the man's voice, but her heart leapt to her throat. The spell, she thought, must have worked! Here at her shoulder must be the man she would love. She turned to look, but saw no man. She looked further turning around next to the well, but still saw no person to have spoken to her.

"Where are you?" she asked.

"Why, right in front of you," said the voice. Monette looked in the direction of the voice and saw only a duck.

"You are a duck!" she exclaimed.

"You are a girl!" the duck spoke back. "I won't hold it against you."

"How is it that you can speak?" she asked.

"There is a powerful enchantment upon me," said the duck. "How is it that you can hear me? I have spoken to every maiden that has come to this well in these ten years. You are the first to hear my voice."

"An enchanted prince!" the silly girl exclaimed. "You must be the one to show me true love."

"I can do that," answered the duck.

"Shall I kiss you?" she asked.

"Ick!" said the duck. "Why would you want to do that?"

"Is it not love's first kiss that will free you from your enchantment?" she asked.

All the stories she had heard worked that way. You find an enchanted prince, kiss him, he returns to his handsome self, and he takes you away to his castle. But the duck had other ideas.

"No. Alas, it is not a kiss that will free me from my enchantment," spoke the duck. "Though I appreciate the offer," he added.

Monette was just a tiny bit relieved.

"What must we do then?" she asked.

"Long ago, a witch put this spell on me," said the duck. "She said that I would remain under the spell until a maiden could look at me and see me for who I really am. It is a dreadful curse, for when maidens see me, they scream and run away. If I am lucky, they miss me with the stone they throw in my direction. Oh, I yearn to return to life as I knew it before the witch cast this evil spell."

Monette had visions of the handsome man she knew must be hidden in the duck, of his castle and wealth, and of the envy of her friends when she married him. But when she looked at the duck, she saw only a talking duck. She could not imagine him changing shape.

"Oh, oh," she moaned. "I can't do it. Tell me what I must do to free you from this dreadful enchantment?"

"In these ten years sitting by the well," said the duck, "I have learned that there is a garment that one might wear, which will show the true nature of what she sees. If you were to wear that garment, I am sure you could see me as I really am and the enchantment would be broken."

"I will find this garment and put it on," said Monette. "What is it?"

"Well, it is a very special vest made from the skin of a lamb," said the duck. "It is not just any sheepskin. This particular lamb was doomed at birth. It grew so fast that its poor body could not stand the stress and it died soon after its first wool came in. So soft was this wool, however, that when the poor creature died, the shepherd lovingly removed its skin, prepared it, and made it into a vest that he wears to this very day."

"Soren's vest?" Monette exclaimed in disbelief and a little disgust. "I need to wear Soren's vest?"

"Ah, so you know the man," said the duck. "He is a fine man who takes loving care of animals, and when this overgrown lamb died, he was so sad that he decided to keep the lamb's skin close to his own for as long as he lived.

It seems the same old witch that cast her spell on me was moved by the sentimental boy and enchanted the animal skin so that the wearer could see truly. I don't think the boy knows what he has, but he has always been a great judge of people. That is the vest you must wear in order to see me as I truly am."

These words came as a shock to Monette. She had sent Soren away from her, asking him to never come again, just that morning. But she supposed the pest would never listen to her. He would certainly be back soon.

"I will find some way to get his vest from him," she vowed. "Then I will look at you and break your enchantment." The duck thanked her and waddled away while Monette went to ponder how she would get the vest from Soren.

True to form, the sheep farmer showed up after his chores were done in the morning to woo the self-centered girl. But this morning Monette seemed more interested in their conversation. She laughed at his gentle humor and then invited him to come back for dinner in the evening.

Soren felt he was being manipulated a bit, but he was happy to return for her company. After dinner, Monette suggested they go for a walk. It was a chilly evening, but Monette conveniently forgot her shawl. By the time she and Soren had walked through the village and had returned to the well, Monette was suffering with the cold. She paused by the well and looked for the duck. There he was.

"I see you have brought the vest," said the duck. "But how are you to get it off?" Monette was shocked by the voice, placing her finger to her lips to hush him. Just then a chill wind blew up and she shivered. Soren lovingly placed his arm around her shoulders to warm her.

"We should go in to the fire," Soren said. "You are cold, Monette."

"Oh, Soren," she answered. "It is so cold out I don't think I can make it back to the house. Please lend me your vest to keep me warm while we walk back."

Soren, being such a kind person as he was, did not hesitate to remove the vest and place it over her shoulders. Monette shivered in glee.

The first thing she noticed was how warm the vest was. The second was how it smelled pleasantly of Soren. The third was that the duck was still a duck.

"It's just a duck," Monette said aloud.

"Yes, it's a duck," Soren said, noticing the animal for the first time.

"Quack," said the duck.

Monette was instantly heartbroken. She had seen the duck as a handsome prince, ready to carry her away. But when she wore the vest of truth, she saw it was really only a duck. The duck seemed quite happy to splash in a pond and come up with a small fish in her mouth.

She turned to Soren and looked at him. He was really very handsome, strong, and certainly kind. His splotchy skin she suddenly saw as colorful. His care for the animals was evidence of his good nature. Most of all, she could see how he truly loved her and cared for her. How was it she had never seen him in this way before? She glanced back at the duck, waddling away. So, this was what it was like to see things as they really were.

She stood on her tiptoes and kissed Soren.

That vest of truth that lets one see things as they really are is the vest I wear today.

13
Fisherman

STEVEN ROSE EARLY and was out of the home of the weaver and the spinner, striding away on the road toward Rich Reach, before the cock crowed. He wanted no more of the dour Weaver, and was completely exhausted by the jovial spinner. He tried to mimic Sergeant's marching rhythm, tapping out the pace on his hip with his hand while he marched away down the road.

Since he was now more than fifty thousand steps from the city, the distances between towns and villages grew longer. Steven saw fewer people on the road. Those he saw were going as quickly as they could from one village to another, or to the castle. Occasionally, Steven glanced over his shoulder and imagined that he could still see the flag at the top of the King's castle.

Soon, Steven settled into a smooth and even one hundred ten steps per minute pace, and since the road was well-maintained and level, he covered ground at an amazing pace. By the end of the day, he had covered another forty thousand steps and was tired. But there was no village here to rest in. He set up a small camp for the night and continued in the morning.

The land began to rise and Steven realized he would be going into the mountains soon. He kept walking all day, lunching on the sandwich the King's cook had given him. At last Steven came to a small town and found the Old Rooster Inn. The town was quiet and at sundown, the streets were empty. When Steven walked into the Inn, the tiny common room—where a dozen people sat drinking—fell deathly silent. Steven cheerfully hailed the innkeeper and asked for a room for the night.

"And who would be asking for a room?" growled the innkeeper. Steven was surprised. All the hostellers he had ever met had been friendly and happy to have guests.

"I'm Steven George the Dragonslayer, on a quest from King Montague Magnus to the Principality of Rich Reach," Steven said brightly.

"You're going to Rich Reach, eh?" said the innkeeper. He turned to the other patrons in the Inn. "He's going to Rich Reach," the innkeeper announced. There was a moment's stunned silence followed by a sudden outburst of laughter. "All these folks are going to Rich Reach," the innkeeper said. "When it's safe."

"Oh," said Steven, looking at the travelers. "I'm going tomorrow."

The laughter fell silent again. The people in the common room glanced at each other, then rose and slipped off to their rooms. In a moment, Steven was alone with the innkeeper.

"You can throw your bedroll over near the fire. I have no other rooms since those who are here keep staying. They are afraid that I'll give another guest their room, so they all hurried off to guard it," the innkeeper said. "You have coins for dinner?"

Steven reached in his pocket and pulled out a gold coin. He looked at it a little surprised, but handed it to the innkeeper. The innkeeper went to get Steven some food and drink while Steven spread out his bedroll by the fire.

When the Innkeeper returned with food and ale, Steven asked why none of the people were continuing on to Rich Reach.

"Well," said the Innkeeper, "there's a darkness on that road. Some time ago people stopped coming from Rich Reach. No one that went from here to there ever returned. So, people stopped going. Then there's the bridge."

Steven had learned a great deal while traveling the road with Selah for seven years and was not the same naïve fellow who started his first quest. He had seen bridges—well one, at least—that spanned a river. No matter what a certain melon farmer had to say, Steven saw no threats in bridges.

"But what is the problem with the bridge?" Steven asked.

"Burned," answered the Innkeeper. "You see, when people saw that no one was coming over the bridge, they began to fear what *might* come over it. Eventually, the fear of what *might* come overwhelmed the prospect of actually crossing themselves, so they burned the bridge."

Steven had begun to sense a growing atmosphere of fear along the road, but had met so few people that he had not been able to examine it. Those he met were all headed toward the King's castle, and were in a great hurry and unwilling to talk. But thinking that he might have to wade or swim across a river was truly discouraging news.

"Is there no other way across?" asked Steven

The Innkeeper glanced around to be sure they were still alone.

"Are you really from the King?" asked the Innkeeper.

Steven reached in his pocket and pulled out the tiny flag the King had given him.

"All right," said the Innkeeper. "Now, not many people know this. They have willingly forgotten. But downstream there is a strange old fisherman named Tavis. I'm told he could get you across the river if you really need to get across the river."

"Where do I find this Tavis?" Steven asked.

"Tomorrow morning, you leave here early so none of the other guests see you go. They'd try to stop you. Keep walking on the main road until you get to the river. You will know you are there when you see the burned-out bridge. Head downstream along the river for a good two-days' walk, maybe more, and you will reach the sea. There, where the river meets the sea, Tavis plies his craft. He has a boat and if it pleases him, he might take you across the river."

"All the way south to the sea?" Steven asked, amazed.

"It's not so far from here as it is from the Castle," the Innkeeper said. "Now you could go upstream and try to cross where it is shallower, but there's a waterfall a day's walk upstream that is an awful hard thing to get around. You'd best go south."

Steven thanked the Innkeeper for his advice and directions, finished his dinner, and then crawled into his bedroll. It seemed so strange to be in an inn with no rooms and no people in the common room. He had a fitful sleep, rose early in the morning, and slipped out of the inn.

AT THE OUTSKIRTS of town, Steven came to the bridge across a river almost as wide as the river near his home. In the midst of the river were the burned out pylons of an old bridge. The far side of the river was hidden in mist in the early morning light. As Steven stood staring at the burned bridge a figure approached from the village.

"It's a shame, isn't it?" said the figure.

Steven jumped. He turned to the person. Steven could not discern whether the speaker, draped in a shapeless robe, was male or female. The voice was that indecipherable tone that belongs to old people and renders gender insignificant.

"I don't know," said Steven honestly. "Did anyone use the bridge?"

"Oh, yes!" the old person said. "After it was built, we discovered it was the most direct route to get to Rich Reach. Of course, when we built it, no one knew that."

"Why did you build it, then?" asked Steven

"For the melons, of course," said the draped figure. "They were never that good, though. I remember when the melons were famous. Such a shame. Perhaps it is better this way."

"What is the name of this place," Steven asked.

"This is the village that was the town that was the City of Tornlace." The old person turned and tottered back toward town.

Seeing the most direct route to his destination cut off, Steven muttered to himself, "Bridges are a great barrier to commerce," and turned to find the path along the river that led downstream.

FOR A DAY, the way was easy going, and Steven met a traveler or two along the path. These were quiet, however, and barely nodded acknowledgment as Steven passed. The second day, the path grew narrow and there were no travelers. Twice Steven stepped into sinkholes that threatened to swallow him as they had swallowed the path before him.

The third day, the terrain changed and Steven had to backtrack several times to be sure he had taken the right path into the swampy land of the delta. But at the end of the third day, when Steven was 285,132 steps from where he parted from Selah, he saw the cabin of Tavis the fisherman. He approached slowly and hailed the owner while he was still several steps away.

"Tavis the Fisherman," Steven called. "I am Steven George the Dragonslayer and I come to you for passage to the other side of the river. Hail, Tavis the Fisherman!"

There was no answer.

Steven advanced a dozen steps and called out again, thinking the fisherman had not heard him. It was just past sunset and darkness was descending rapidly around the cabin.

Again, there was no answer.

Steven stood, debating whether he should approach the cabin. He had just decided he had no other choice when a soft touch brushed against his shoulder and a voice whispered.

"Wooooo. Whooooo comes in the night?"

"Ah, Master Fisherman," Steven said turning. The Fisherman was so startled by Steven turning to address him that he stumbled backward and fell over a fallen log. "Let me help you to your feet," said Steven, reaching out his hand.

"You startled me," said Tavis. "No one has ever turned to talk to me!"

"Why would I do anything else?" asked Steven. "I was calling to you. Why would you not answer?"

"Now that is a good question," said the Fisherman. "Why would I not answer?"

"Shall we go inside and discuss the matter?" Steven asked.

"Yes. Let's do that. Thank you for the invitation," said the Fisherman.

Once inside the Fisherman's cabin, Steven found everything as normal as he could expect from a man who snuck up on visitors and tried to scare them. Inside the cabin, the fisherman seemed to suddenly remember this was his home and set about stoking the fire. Other than that, he seemed no more normal than the Innkeeper from whom Steven had last had hospitality, or the strange old person by the river.

When he thought about that, Steven wondered if it was he himself who was not acting normal.

"Did you come from Tornlace?" asked the fisherman.

"Yes," said Steven.

"Did they tell you I would help you?" asked Tavis.

"The innkeeper said you *might* help me get to the other side of the river," Steven answered, uncertainly.

"Ah ha!" declared the Fisherman as if he had just found the flaw in Steven's logic. "And you felt that this allusion to help was adequate for you to walk three days through darkness and treacherous unknowns, find yourself alone in a dark swamp, and shout out to a man you have never met to give you help?"

"Well, yes," said Steven.

"Okay. That makes sense," said the fisherman. "How can I help you?"

Steven thought he'd been clear, but restated his request.

"I would like you to ferry me to the other side of the river," said Steven. "I am commissioned by the King to find and master the Terror of Rich Reach."

"You don't think I'm the Terror?"

"You are just a Fisherman," said Steven.

"Let's not be insulting," said Tavis. "I'm very proud to be a fisherman."

"Why do you try to scare people who come to visit you, then?" Steven asked.

"I tell you what," the Fisherman said. He looked around and leaned closer to Steven conspiratorially across the fireplace. "I'll tell you a story if you'll tell me one."

Steven readily agreed. The Fisherman poured each of them a glass of wine and settled on the opposite side of the fire to tell his story.

14
The Silver Scale

ONCE UPON A TIME, when most of the world was covered by water and only islands had dry land, there was a poor fisherman named Carpface, who lived on his boat with his nets and scaling knives and little else. He fished the waters of the great sea, trading his catch on docks of the various islands that he came to.

It was a time when the world was still filled with mystery and new discoveries. Carpface heard stories of new wonders each time he docked at the islands, but he never imagined that he would experience one of these wonders himself.

So, it was a surprise to Carpface when on a night with a sliver of moon for light, as he plied his nets in a deep lagoon, he heard a voice from the water.

"Help me! Help me!" said the voice. "I don't want to come from the water. Let me go!"

Carpface looked around to find out who was calling to him. He was alone on the water for as far as the eye could see. But when the voice came again, he looked down at his nets. There, caught in the web, was a silver fish, whose scales shone in the faint moonlight. The fish was so beautiful that it made Carpface gasp for breath. But most amazing was the voice coming from the fish.

"Please don't take me away from the clear blue waters of the sea!" begged the fish. "Let me go and I will give you amazing good fortune."

"What a wonder!" said Carpface. "I never thought to see such a thing. My fortune could be made by taking this amazing fish to the villages. People would give me a great house because Carpface has a talking fish with silver scales!"

At this, the fish thrashed desperately in the net.

"This I will give to you and more," said the fish. "I will give to you a wife and wealth and a home and more, if only you will leave me in the sea."

Carpface considered this.

"But how am I to know this?" asked Carpface. "If I let you go in the sea, I will have nothing. You will swim away and I will continue to spend my life a poor soul without so much as a story to tell."

"Fisherman," said the silver fish, "this is how you will prove you have seen me. Take one of my silver scales. You can show people the scale to prove that you saw me. But my scales are more than pure silver. If you dip the scale in the sea, I will come to you."

Now, Carpface was a simple man, but he was basically good of heart. He believed the fish, and having plucked a silver scale from its side, he set it free in the deep sea. No sooner had the fish slipped away than Carpface's nets were overwhelmed with a catch of fish larger than any he had seen before. He struggled to haul his nets and the fish into the boat, almost swamping it, and rowed the foundering craft to the nearest island.

It was daybreak when Carpface reached the docks. People were standing at the shore and all the other boats had docked before him. Carpface despaired that he was the last to reach the dock and that people would all have bought their fish from the other fishermen before he got there.

But when he beached his boat, he discovered quite the opposite. For the fifth day in a row all the fishing boats for this island had come back empty. The people were becoming desperate for food and were near rioting against the fishermen. But when Carpface arrived with a boat laden with fish, the angry crowds calmed.

The other fishermen rushed to help Carpface with his haul and he was treated as a savior for both the people and the fishermen. When the fish had all been sold or traded, Carpface had more money than he had ever seen before. The fishermen all wanted to know where he had made such a fine catch. The innkeeper gave Carpface his best room and a meal made of his own fish. Carpface was a hero.

After he had eaten a fish-filled breakfast in the morning, Carpface walked out along the beach near the village. When he was alone, he pulled the silver scale from his pocket and dipped it in the sea. In only a moment, the water churned and the silver fish appeared a few feet away.

"What is it you want?" asked the fish.

"Why, I only wanted to thank you," said Carpface. "I have sold a great number of fish and am now a wealthy man. The catch I made after I set you free saved this island from starvation. I am truly grateful to you."

"And you called me just to thank me?" asked the fish.

"Yes, sir fish. I am a humble fisherman. You have made me a gentleman," answered Carpface sincerely.

"Then you shall have more," said the fish. "I am not finished yet."

The fish disappeared beneath the waves and suddenly Carpface heard a distant scream. He looked around and saw a young woman on a spit of land some ways away. She had been gathering clams when the tide turned. Now, she was wholly surrounded by the sea that closed in on her rapidly.

Carpface did not stop to think, but dove into the waters and swam to reach the woman. He picked her up in his arms and carried her to safety with his strong strokes. When they had reached the safety of the beach, he set her gently on the sand.

"You are the bravest of men," said the young woman. "I will take you to my father so you can be rewarded for saving me."

With that, she led Carpface to the finest house in the town. Her father, as it happened, was the wealthiest man on the island, and was deemed both a wise man and a prince. When he heard what his daughter had to say about how Carpface bravely swam the sea to rescue her, and saw the way his daughter looked at the fisherman, the prince made his judgment.

"Carpface the Fisherman," he said, "you have saved our town from starvation and now you have saved my daughter. It is only fitting that you should be rewarded according to your bravery and your unselfishness. You shall have the hand of my daughter in marriage, and from this day forward you shall be my son and heir to my estates."

It was not long thereafter that Carpface and the young woman were married. He lived in the finest house of the island, and when his father-in-law died, he became the ruler of all the island and people. He, too, grew old and rich with years and happiness, all because of his mercy to the silver fish, and his politeness in thanking it.

YOU MIGHT BELIEVE that Carpface lived happily ever after, and not be far from correct. But when Carpface's son came of age, Carpface decided to tell the story of the silver fish at last. He rose and told all that I have told you now, but people did not believe him. They thought the story was the sign of the dotage of a respected leader. That is when Carpface pulled the silver scale from his pocket and held it so that all could see.

They were amazed. No one had ever seen silver so pure and so brilliant. The silver scale became the talk of the city, and soon the story spread from island to island. This drew strangers to the city that had grown up around Carpface and the little village. The strangers came for no other reason than to see the scale and perhaps to gain it for themselves. And so it happened that as he walked one day by the sea where he had walked so many times before, Carpface was set upon by robbers and was killed. The silver scale disappeared with the attackers. After his death, Carpface was honored and buried by the people and his son ascended the throne.

Over the years, people have whispered about the silver scale and have speculated about where it is and what happened to those who stole it, but only I know what happened next.

The brigands fought among themselves over who would own the silver scale until only one was left. This one set out in a boat and when he was alone on the seas, he dipped the scale in the water. The silver fish that rose to greet the pirate was not a tiny fish like Carpface had seen. Many years had passed and the fish had grown to almost the size of a man.

"Carpface, is that you?" asked the fish.

The pirate was awed by the size of the fish and all the glittering silver scales that covered its body.

"Ah… Greetings Silver Fish," said the pirate as he maneuvered closer. "I bring you news. Your old friend Carpface has died. I have come at his last request to return your silver scale to you." Now the great silver fish was saddened, for Carpface had been kind, grateful, and a good leader for his people.

"Thank you for bringing me this news," said the fish. "And for returning the scale I gave him."

The pirate waited for a reward from the fish, but the fish said nothing further.

"Is that all?" asked the pirate angrily. "Is there no reward for this?"

"What do I owe you for returning that which is mine?" asked the fish.

"Carpface had wealth, family, power," said the brigand. "That is what I would have."

"You are not worthy of these," said the fish, "for I see now that you did not bring me word of these things for any reason but that you caused them to happen. You shall reap the reward of your deeds, just as Carpface reaped wealth and happiness."

At that, the pirate was so angered that he threw the anchor at the great fish and struck him senseless. It was still a great struggle, however, before the brigand was able to kill the silver fish and pull him into his boat. He greedily began to strip the fish of the silver scales, declaring over and over that he was now rich and would be a great man with the silver of the fish's scales.

But this was an age of wonders, and the wonders were not over yet. The pirate scarcely noticed that as he stripped the scales from the great fish, they clung to his hands and then his arms. In his greedy scaling of the fish, he scarcely noticed that the scales covered his face and his body. And when he finished scaling the fish and had dumped the body overboard, he looked around him and saw only one silver scale left in the boat, for the rest coated his own body.

Now, looking at his hands and body, he began to itch and yearn for a bath in the sea. He dove into the water and disappeared. For all that had happened, only one silver scale was left.

You might ask how I know this part of the tale. It is because I have that silver scale, and I have spoken to the great silver fish and heard his story. Any man who catches and kills the silver fish is cursed to become him in his turn.

STEVEN WATCHED AS Tavis the Fisherman removed a leather pouch from his waist and emptied its contents into his hand. There lay one large silver fish scale. This, the fisherman handed to Steven.

"It is yours now," said the fisherman. "As I get older, I get more tempted to use it to call the fish and take its wealth for my own. But that path is doom for a fisherman. Perhaps you will find a better way."

Steven began to protest, but when he looked up at the fisherman, he found him sound asleep. Steven dropped the scale in his pocket and drifted off to sleep himself. In the morning, he told his story to Tavis the Fisherman.

15
The Grain of Salt

ONCE UPON A TIME, in the darkness of night, a poor widow stood by her fire in her little hovel despairing that she would ever eat again. Her food was gone and winter was approaching. She searched every corner of her little hut, but all she found was a grain of salt.

"Oh," said the widow to herself, "how good this grain of salt would be on a nice haunch of venison. What a savory stew it would make with some vegetables and a rabbit. How it would bring out the flavor of a nice fat goose. How it would help the yeast raise a nice loaf of bread. But alas, I have only this grain of salt and no venison, no vegetables, no rabbit, no goose, and no flour. I shall starve with naught but this grain of salt."

The old widow wept, and her wailing was heard by a passing tinker who happened that way.

The tinker was moved with pity for the old woman and when she had told her tale, he, too, sat with her and wept. The noise of the two crying out attracted the attention of a farmer who stopped to see what the problem was.

"I have no venison, no vegetables, no rabbits, no goose, and no flour," cried the old woman. "I have only this grain of salt and I shall starve." Hearing her tale of woe, the farmer, too, sat down to weep. Soon a miller happened upon the trio, and when he had heard the sorry tale, he sat to weep with the woman, the tinker, and the farmer.

Now it happened that a soldier was passing nearby and he heard the wailing. In spite of the fact that he had been marching for several days on only his rations and had recently run out of all but a few beans, the soldier responded to the sound of citizens in distress. He rushed to the old woman's house, prepared to stave off bandits or enemy soldiers. But he found the widow, the farmer, the tinker, and the miller all weeping about the sorry state of poverty that the widow endured.

The soldier was a clever man who had fought in many wars, and had honored his king in many ways. He had seen poverty and been near starvation; he had faced death and commanded men. And when he saw the weeping people, he thought to himself that he had never seen such foolishness. But in his wisdom, he said nothing of this. Instead, he comforted the four.

"I know something of starvation," he said, "and I was just this moment looking for a good meal. But since you are so poor, I will share an army secret with you. I will show you all how to make salt soup, and then we will all feast and our bellies will be filled."

The widow, the tinker, the farmer, and the miller were all amazed. They had never heard of such a thing as salt soup. Was it possible that they would survive after all? They paid careful attention to the instructions the soldier gave and instantly obeyed his voice of command.

"Now," said the soldier, "we shall need a pot." The widow brought the soldier her tiny kettle.

The tinker looked at the widow's tiny pot and quickly said, "That pot will never hold enough soup for all of us. I have a much larger pot in my wagon." With that, he left and returned with a large kettle that they filled with water and put on the fire.

The soldier tasted the soup and smacked his lips with satisfaction. "There is a secret to making this type of soup," the soldier said. "We must cover the kettle with a sheepskin to hold in the flavor." Now the widow had a tiny scrap of sheepskin that she used to keep her warm at night, and no matter how they tugged at it, it was not large enough to cover the kettle. That is when the farmer jumped up.

"I have a sheep I was planning to butcher," the farmer said. "I will bring its skin and we will cover the pot with it. That way we will all learn how to make salt soup and none of us will ever be hungry again." This sounded like a good idea to everyone, but as the farmer left, the soldier spoke to him.

"It would be wonderful if a haunch of mutton accompanied its skin to the pot," he said. "Perhaps you could bring that as well and it will make the salt soup so much better." The farmer quickly agreed and went off to butcher his sheep. While he was gone, the soldier reached in his pocket and pulled out his handful of beans.

"Salt soup is so much better when it has beans and onions in it," said the soldier. "I have only beans, but that will have to do."

"I have an onion," said the miller. "I will fetch it, for when we have learned to make salt soup, none of us will ever go hungry again." As he rose to leave, the soldier called him aside.

"Of course," he said, "carrots would be nice to have, but the onion will have to do."

"I will find a carrot," said the miller enthusiastically, and he rushed off to do so.

Now, other people nearby heard the gathering and saw the farmer, the tinker, and the miller run out on their various errands. When they asked what was happening, they were told that a soldier was teaching them to make salt soup so they would never have to go hungry again. This made the villagers very happy and many came to the doorway of the widow's tiny home and asked if they might learn to make salt soup as well. Each was sent away to gather an herb, a potato, a slice of venison, a loaf of bread, or some other small thing that their pantry would not miss. Soon the kettle was boiling and had been covered with the sheepskin.

Many people gathered outside the widow's home, awaiting a chance to taste the fabulous salt soup. The smells had wafted across the area and by dinner time, everyone was very hungry. At last, the soldier pronounced the soup "ready for the salt."

"The secret," said the soldier, "is to add the salt just before you are ready to serve the soup. If you keep the kettle covered with the sheepskin throughout the cooking process, there will always be enough."

With that, the widow brought forth her solitary grain of salt and the soldier lifted the skin from the top just enough that the widow could cast the grain of salt into the kettle. The instant burst of aroma that flooded the widow's home and the surrounding area was so wonderful and so intense that the entire village swooned. Then the soldier began to dip the soup into the bowls of the waiting people, starting with the widow who took the first sip of the soup.

"This is amazing!" said the widow. "To think that all I needed to make this delicious soup was one grain of salt!" Each person who tasted the soup agreed and all were thrilled with the new recipe.

"To make salt soup successfully," said the soldier, when at last he had tasted the soup himself, "you must all come together. No one person can eat a kettle of soup so delicious. But when you all share in the making and the eating, there will be plenty."

"Now we shall never be hungry again," exclaimed the widow.

You may think this a strange tale, but I have made salt soup on many occasions, and this sheepskin vest I wear is the cover for my kettle.

16
Silly Geese

THE FISHERMAN WAS PLEASED with the story and even examined Steven's vest to affirm that there was a black ring on the inside where it had been held to a kettle.

"Salt soup, salt soup," the fisherman said over and over. "I must find some people with whom to make salt soup. I shall have to go back to the village of Tornlace and get the innkeeper to join me in making salt soup. Yes, that is what I will do. There is a farmer who will join me. And the blacksmith. We will have a feast of salt soup."

He took Steven out of his house into the morning sun and led him to his boat. It did not look like much, and Steven wondered if it floated at all. It was broad and flat-bottomed. Though it seemed not to sit deeply in the water, the sides were high and it did appear that a large catch could be held in its hold.

"Have you ever filled the boat with fish?" Steven asked.

"Well now, not for many years," said the fisherman. "Time was that Tornlace was a thriving town, even a city. Every week I would pole my boat up the mouth of the river to the village and sell as many fish as I could catch. There is no sense in catching so many fish now that I cannot sell them. I'm happy to catch my dinner, and once every several days, dock at the burned out bridge to supply those who remain in the village."

"What happened to the village?" Steven asked.

"The Terror," Tavis answered. "After the melons gave out, people began to move back to the village from the far side of the river. Soon there was no one living on the other side. It was still a main route of travel to Rich Reach, but people gradually lost interest in going there. Came a time when you looked across the river and it looked like there were shadows walking among the deserted houses on the other side."

"But there were no ghosts. The people had moved!" Steven said.

"Aye, but then we got word that something was terrorizing Rich Reach and the people burned the bridge to keep whatever it was away from their village. Problem was, with no bridge, there was no longer a reason to come through Tornlace at all. When people stopped coming *through* the town, they stopped coming *to* the town. Someday there will be nothing left there but the burned pylons of the bridge, warning people not to cross the river."

"That's sad," said Steven. "Have you tried to sell fish to other villages?"

"Other villages either have their fishermen or are too far away from the water to get fish," scoffed Tavis. "What I'm going to do is find me a magic fish and make a wish. He must be around here somewhere. Now what did I do with that scale?"

Steven almost told him that he'd given it to him, but the fisherman had genuinely feared his greed overwhelming him and killing the silver fish. He kept his mouth shut.

"How far is it to the other side of the river?" Steven asked, realizing they were nowhere near shore.

"Oh, I can't take you straight across the river," the fisherman said. "There is no place to dock my boat in the swamps, and you would be unable to walk. There is a smaller channel that cuts up farther along the seashore. If I let you off there, you'll be able to find your way back to the road to Rich Reach… if it still exists."

Steven contemplated the possibility that the road to Rich Reach might not exist anymore. If that were the case, how would he ever find the principality? Well, as was always the case, Steven assumed that all roads would ultimately lead to where he was supposed to be. They had all led to his dragon. They would all lead to his Terror, if he was meant to face it.

At long last, Tavis pointed the boat toward shore and Steven gradually began to see the shape of a small river mouth indenting the shoreline. Into this river, Tavis expertly guided the boat. Just as they passed the shoreline, Steven saw a drake and his hen, floating in the current just to port. He pointed toward them.

"Duck," said Tavis.

"Two of them," answered Steven.

"No, duck!" the fisherman yelled, pointing forward. Steven turned to follow the fisherman's gesture and was smacked squarely in the head by a heavy low-hanging tree limb. It knocked the breath from Steven and Steven from the boat. Water closed over the top of him and all went dark as the current swept him away.

WHEN STEVEN AWOKE, he had difficulty remembering where he was. He was lying on a bed of straw, covered with warm wool blankets. Not far away he could hear a gentle female voice humming a little tune that seemed vaguely familiar to him. There was a scent in the air of drying sheepskin and Steven could just make out his vest, lying over an iron kettle to dry. He realized suddenly that all his clothes were draped over chairs, table, and mantel, and then the most beautiful visage Steven had ever seen came into view.

"Selah?" he asked, hesitantly, trying to clear his eyes.

"What is that, my fine funny fish?" the woman asked, coming toward him. Steven realized his mistake at once. This was not Selah. With that realization, Steven adjusted his opinion of her beauty downward. No doubt there was beautiful, and there was Madame Selah Welinska. They could not be compared. This woman was merely more beautiful than any non-dragon lady Steven had ever met.

"I'm sorry," he said. "I thought you were someone else."

"A wonder you can think at all with that knot on your head," the woman said, good-naturedly. Steven felt his head and found a bandage that covered part of his forehead. Then he felt further and discovered that his hair had been cut short and his beard had been shaved smooth.

"I had to trim your hair away from the area that I bandaged," explained the woman. "It seemed silly to only barber a portion of your head without doing the whole thing."

"I seem to have no clothes on," said Steven shyly.

"Well, I wasn't going to put you beneath clean blankets in seawater soaked clothes," said the woman. "I wasn't even sure there was a man in that bundle of rags when I pulled you out of my net."

"Are you a fisherwoman?" Steven asked.

"I am a woman who fishes," she answered. "I also hunt, farm, weave, cook and build."

"Who are you?" Steven asked, bluntly.

"I am Cherissé," she answered. "And who are you?"

"Oh, my apologies," Steven said. "I am Steven George the Dragonslayer."

"Such a mighty name for such a bedraggled fish!" laughed the woman. "Did you get hit by your dragon's tail? Did he burn your charger and melt your armor?" She was clearly having a good time ridiculing Steven, so he very politely let her continue. "Was it an underwater dragon? A sea monster? From what mountain did your dragon throw you that you would end up in the sea?"

"The dragon was a long time ago," Steven answered quietly. "I am on another quest now."

"Ah. A quest," she nodded knowingly. Steven had a difficult time focusing on what she was saying as she gently removed his bandage and cleaned his wound with fresh water. "What would you be questing for?" she mused. "The golden fleece? The Holy Grail? The One Ring? The Fountain of Youth? The Meaning of Life? Dear me, there are so many things on which one might waste one's life."

"The Terror," said Steven simply.

"What foolishness," said Cherissé. "Certainly, there must be enough terror in life to go around without seeking it out. People generally make their own terror, flee from it, and blame it for all the world's ills. Few face it and certainly, no one seeks it."

"I do," Steven answered. Something about Cherissé caused him to be subdued and quiet. He could scarcely put more than two words together.

"Well, you will be questing after nothing for a time, my hero," Cherissé said mockingly. "You must stay abed and let my medicines work on your wound. Here, let me feed you some stew so that you may gain back your strength."

Steven found himself lulled by her soothing voice, and comforted by her gentle hands. He ate the stew hungrily.

In fact, he could not remember having tasted such a savory mix before. He tried to identify the flavor. When he asked, Cherissé answered simply, "Goose."

Cherissé went about her business as Steven watched sleepily from the blankets by the fire. He did manage to remove his vest from the kettle before it was cooked. It would take some work to clean the fur before it was fit to wear again. Cherissé washed Steven's other clothes and hung them to dry, then went out to feed her "pets," as she called them. Steven could hear the honking of the geese as they gathered around her. When Cherissé returned, she checked Steven's head wound and he felt her cool hand against his hot skin.

"You must rest, my Dragonslayer," Cherissé said. "You are not strong enough to quest. We can entertain ourselves with stories as you mend," she added.

"Do you mean to Once Upon a Time me?" Steven asked.

"Well," she answered seductively, "I suppose once would not hurt." Then she stood from where she knelt beside him and said simply, "But not tonight. You are not well enough yet and the medicine has not had a chance to work. Go to sleep. You will feel better in the morning."

And Steven slept.

THE NEXT DAY, Steven sat up on his bed of straw and Cherissé handed him his clothes, which he donned beneath the wool blankets. Cherissé made everything he did and thought seem like it shouldn't be done. It was a new feeling for Steven, and he did not know how to describe it. He was not at all comfortable with the hot redness that touched his cheeks whenever he glanced in the direction of Cherissé or felt her hand touch his brow.

By afternoon, however, Steven was able to stand and he joined Cherissé in feeding her geese. The flock seemed oddly tame and Cherissé called each goose by name as it came to rub its cheek against her hand and take the offered food. The calls of the geese seemed oddly plaintive and made Steven homesick for his own village that he had left so long ago.

"Such unusual names you have for your geese," said Steven. "It is almost as if they were people one might meet on the road."

"One never knows what one might meet on the road," replied Cherissé. "Perhaps a goose has spoken to you as you journeyed and you failed to hear its voice. There are certainly enough people you might meet who are little more than silly geese."

After they had eaten and Cherissé had changed Steven's bandages again, they sat together companionably in front of the fire as Steven began to work the tangles out of the fleece vest with a brush he drew from its pocket.

"Well, then," said Cherissé. "Shall we begin?" She smiled and Steven nodded. Then Cherissé began her story.

17
The Bowl of Light

ONCE UPON A TIME, there was a blind man who walked in darkness all his life. He had been blind from birth and had learned how to cope with his life. In fact, he functioned so well, that upon first meeting him, you would scarcely know he was blind.

He ran his own farm. He milked his own cows. He raised his own chickens. He cooked his own meals. All things that a man would normally do for himself, Rodda the Dark did for himself. And if, occasionally, his choice of clothes did not measure up to the standards of the sighted, or if he missed a bit of his face while shaving, those around him accepted him as one of themselves, and the fact that he was blind was nearly forgotten.

Forgotten, that is, by all but Rhodda the Dark. While Rhodda accepted his blindness and made the best of his life, there was always one thing he could not fathom. He did not understand the concept of light.

Rhodda knew how close a person was by the sound of their voice or the echo of their footstep. He knew the shape of his wife by touch as well as he knew his own shape. He knew the feel of heat from the fire and the scent of bread baking. But Rhodda yearned to know what light was. It was the only thing he could not smell, touch, hear, or taste.

Rhodda heard people talk of how light the day was, how the light played tricks on them, the quality of light in a painting, but he did not know what light was.

And thus Rhodda's life would have ended if it were not for a peculiar happening. As Rhodda rode his horse one day, he sensed that one of his cattle had gone astray, and directed the horse with his knees to go and cut it off before it went too far. As the horse wove in and out of the cattle to drive the stray back into the herd, Rhodda sat confidently in the saddle, directing the horse according to what he heard and smelled. In no time at all, the errant beast was back with the herd.

But it was not long before the same animal broke away from the herd again, determined to make it to greener pastures elsewhere. Again, Rhodda guided the horse as expertly as any sighted person could do and drove the calf back to the herd.

When the calf broke from the herd the third time, the horse was more prepared than Rhodda was. Being an expert rider, Rhodda kept his seat on the horse's back, but was unprepared when the horse galloped under a low branch that swept Rhodda from the saddle. He landed hard on the ground and struck his head a sound blow on a rock where he landed. Such a blow might have killed some men, but Rhodda was found by a laborer and was carried to his home. His wife nursed him back to health, through fever and delirium.

Then one morning Rhodda opened his eyes.

A new sensation washed over him. He could see his wife before him twice. Once was as he always saw her, with his nose, his hands, and his ears. And once was with his eyes.

It was a disorienting sensation. He saw everything as he normally 'saw' it, with his other senses, but now he was with his eyes as well. The double 'vision' made it difficult for Rhodda to judge where he was, how far a person was from him, and even where the step was on the ladder he climbed to the loft every day. He often closed his eyes so he could 'see' normally.

The town near Rhodda's farm held a great celebration of Rhodda's miraculous healing. Rhodda's wife was thrilled with the news that he could see her and see their children, but Rhodda was miserable. For all that he had his full senses, he found it harder to do his work, and he knew in his heart that something was missing. Rhodda could not see the light.

Rhodda went to the town hall where a great artwork hung. He had listened to people comment about the light in the picture. Rhodda had gone over every inch of the painting with his fingertips and knew every brush stroke. He thought, surely now he would be able to see the light in the painting. But when Rhodda looked at the painting, he saw only the brushstrokes that he had long before felt and memorized. He simply could not see 'the light.'

At night, he could see the moon and the stars, but could not identify the light. In the daytime, he could see the horse and cattle. He could tell when he had clothes of the same color. He saw his children run to play. But he could not see the light.

"Where, oh where," Rhodda moaned, "is the light? Have people played a cruel joke on me? Why can I not see the light?" Rhodda was miserable. He began to wear a cloth tied around his eyes so he would no longer be confused by his extra sense. People were sad for Rhodda, and the poor man became more and more reclusive.

Still, Rhodda tried to maintain his work, his farm, and his family. He rode out on his horse each day, but as soon as he was out of sight from his house, he tied the blindfold over his eyes. And each day he rode farther away from his home. One day, he failed to return at all.

Rhodda had begun his quest for the light, and he never turned back.

For many years, there were rumors of the blindfolded horseman who rode all the trails of the world searching for light. He was said to have shown up in this village, or to have ridden through that city. But wherever he went, he asked the same question: "Can you show me the light?"

Now in the village of Grand Upman, there was an old madman. When he was a young madman, people were disturbed by his presence and feared his insanity. Children tormented him and adults shunned him, and more than one dog bit him. But as he grew older, he became commonplace. People ceased to notice him or his madness because he was always there. Even the dogs ignored him.

It was the habit of this madman to take his stone bowl to the river each day and polish it with sand. He did this until the bowl was worn so thin and was polished so brightly that it reflected everything that was seen in it. Of course, the people of Grand Upman did not notice the condition of the stone bowl.

What the people of Grand Upman also ceased to notice was that after the madman had polished his bowl, he would hold the bowl in his cupped hands, and after a few moments, rush with the bowl, carefully to the stable where he slept, and pretend to pour the contents of the bowl into a rain barrel. No one noticed and no one cared.

What the madman saw was that when he held the bowl just so on a sunny day, it filled with the light of the sun, reflected off its glassy surface. This bowl of light, he quickly carried to the rain barrel, lifted the lid, and poured in.

Then he clamped the lid down again. But the madman always complained that the rain barrel leaked, because whenever he went for some light on a sunless day, the barrel would be empty. This did not deter him, however, from running from the stream to the rain barrel several times each sunny day to save light for the winter.

One day, as was perhaps inevitable, the blind horseman met the madman of Grand Upman. Not knowing it was a madman, the blind man stopped near when he heard a voice chanting, "A bowl of light. A bowl of light. Save it for a rainy day. A bowl of light."

Rhodda slid wearily from his old horse and lifted the blindfold from his eyes. His senses were assaulted by all the visual input and it took him a moment before he could focus on the madman and his bowl.

"Friend," said Rhodda, "do you have a bowl of light?"

"Oh yes," said the madman. "A bowl of light. A bowl of light. Save it for a rainy day. A bowl of light."

Rhodda began to weep and the tears clouded the vision of his eyes.

"Can you show me the light?" begged Rhodda.

The old madman was so surprised at someone asking him a 'sensible' question that he stopped what he was doing and looked at Rhodda. He saw someone he felt was nearly as mad as he was.

"Yes, stranger," said the madman. "Come look. I have a bowl of light right here, come look." Rhodda made his way to the madman and stood beside him. "Take my bowl and look into it. It is filled with light!" the madman exclaimed.

Rhodda took the bowl and held it in his hands, peering into its shiny depths. He sighed heavily, and then he saw it. The sun reflected off of every surface of the polished bowl, piercing into Rhodda's eyes. It hurt to look at it, but at last Rhodda knew he was seeing the light. The bowl held his eyes captive and Rhodda stared without blinking all afternoon. When at last Rhodda handed the bowl back to the madman and looked around him, all he could see was the light. The maddening images that had kept him confused and off-balance since he had gained his sight were gone. All that was left was the light—bright, unchanging, blinding light.

Rhodda thanked the madman profusely. He remounted his horse and rode back to his farm. He greeted his wife with his eyes wide open. His children had grown, but he recognized them at once. He navigated his farm the way he had always done, without faltering or stumbling.

Everyone thought that Rhodda had finally accepted his sight. But what no one knew was that all he could see with his eyes was the light. He was as blind as the day he was born.

Rhodda lived to a very old age as a very happy man, and it is said that the light never faded from his eyes.

STEVEN WAS MESMERIZED by the sound of Cherissé's voice. He had heard many stories in his life, but few voices like hers. He wanted nothing more than to listen to her speak forever, and understood how Rhodda had felt when he saw the light. Steven slept and awoke the next morning craving the sound of Cherissé's voice. She sent him to feed the geese, to tend her fishing lines, and to cook her food. Each task he did willingly just to hear her give him another. And at evening he came to her with his story.

"What?" Cherissé demanded. "You want to tell a story?"

"I must," said Steven. "I owe you a story."

"But we have a long time for you to pay your story debt," said Cherissé.

"It is only fair that I repay your kindness," said Steven. He was becoming a little unsure of why Cherissé would be so reluctant to have him tell his story.

"Why don't I tell another story, instead?" she said.

This was a great temptation to Steven. To hear the beautiful woman tell another story would be a delight he could not find words for. But Steven's honor dictated that he repay his story debt before incurring more. He could not forget that he still owed Madame Selah Welinska a story that he had yet to pay back. He insisted that he tell a story and at last Cherissé consented.

Steven reached in the pocket of his sheepskin vest and pulled out three balls that he began to toss into the air and catch again.

18
The Balls of Fire

ONCE UPON A TIME, when the world was all in balance, there lived a clever juggler named Nico. He had begun juggling on his mother Mika's farm where he was set to gather the eggs each morning. Nico thought it very clever that he could toss eggs into the air and then catch them without dropping or breaking a single one.

Nico had begun by simply tossing a single egg into the air over and over. One egg might not be missed if he dropped it, so he learned to toss it only so high and to catch it gently. He learned to catch it behind his back and to throw it under his leg and to still snatch it out of the air at exactly the right moment. When Nico had practiced for many days, and had gone a week without dropping an egg, he added a second egg. And so it went until he was able to juggle five eggs without dropping them and to place them all in the basket without an accident.

Nico thought he was very clever and that no one was the wiser for his little entertainments. But the people of the village, to whom Mika sold the eggs, began to notice something strange. Mika's hens, they said, laid scrambled eggs. The eggs became very popular. People began to pass up other egg vendors in the market to take a chance that they would get a scrambled egg from Mika.

Only Nico understood where the scrambled eggs came from, and he had great fun deciding each day if he would scramble three by juggling them, or spend longer fetching the eggs and scramble ten.

Nico's great talent was not destined to stay secret long. One day, Mika sent Nico to the market to trade eggs for peaches so she could make a pie. Nico took a basket of eggs to trade and spoke to the orchard owner about getting peaches.

"Well," said the orchardist, "I have windfall peaches that I would trade for normal eggs, but if I were guaranteed scrambled eggs, I could give you the finest peaches picked from the highest branches of the trees."

The orchardist thought that Nico could not guarantee such a thing, but Nico quickly agreed. He took six large white eggs from his basket and the orchardist selected six of the finest peaches. Then Nico began to juggle.

He had never put six eggs into the air at the same time before, but under the astonished gaze of the orchardist, Nico juggled all the eggs he had brought and kept them in the air until he was content that they could not be anything other than scrambled. Then he gave them to the orchardist, who immediately cracked the eggs one after another into a frying pan and verified that he had received six scrambled eggs. He gave the peaches to Nico, and Mika baked a fine peach pie.

But the secret was out. It was not Mika's hens that laid scrambled eggs, but Nico's juggling that scrambled them.

You might think people would simply want to enjoy the amazing feats of Nico the Juggler. But Nico lived in a very practical community. It was not long before the dairyman came to Nico with three skins of fresh cream to juggle. When Nico had juggled for some time, the dairyman opened the skins to find butter, and gave some to Nico for his labor. Now it became routine for Nico to scramble eggs and to make butter, and for his efforts his mother's farm prospered.

The number of jobs that Nico could do because of his amazing juggling talent seemed limitless. He could knead five loaves of bread at the same time. He could make three pints of butter, and half a dozen scrambled eggs. He could blend the paint for the barn to a perfect hue and scrub four pots at once. Nico was in great demand.

Along with his hands, Nico discovered that his sense of balance was so keen that he could stand on one foot while he used the other to help in his tasks. He might, for example, be scrambling half a dozen eggs with his hands and stirring a cake batter with a spoon held in his toes.

When there was building to be done, Nico set nails for three carpenters at once by using his clever hands and feet. At the dock, Nico could separate a boatload of fish into neat piles of cod, trout, and snapper, then serve the customers by throwing them the fish with one hand and collecting their money with the other.

Perhaps one of Nico's most spectacular feats was performed when the bell rope in the warning tower broke. While attempting to repair it, the watchman slipped through the trapdoor in the tower and fell through the ladder, breaking every rung on his way down.

Nico quickly dragged a cart from the market to the base of the tower and climbed on top of it. It was obvious that he would never reach the top of the tower from the cart, so he called for a table which he piled on top of the cart. Then he stacked chairs in a pyramid and used an old ladder from a nearby loft. By the time Nico was done, he had climbed a rickety stack of furniture and equipment to the height of the tower, attached a new bell rope, and disassembled the stack as he slid down the rope from the top of the tower. He was once again a hero.

Nico's fame began to spread, and as with all things heroic, the stories were greater than the deeds. The story spread that Nico had thrown a rope in the air, shinnied up it while it was still flying, and then tied it to the bell and slid down.

Soon people from surrounding towns came to ask Nico for help. In one town, a child was trapped on the upper floor of a house that caught fire. The bucket brigade was having no luck dousing the flames, so Nico stacked up the buckets, climbed to the window of the burning house, and carried the child down. It was not long before the story spread that Nico had piled water on top of itself to swim to the top of the building.

Since Nico never knew what kind of job he might be called upon to do, or what he might need to do it, he began to sew pockets into his vest so that he could store things that he might need to juggle. He kept eggs in one pocket, cream in another, a knife, string, five smooth sticks, a dozen round stones, and anything he passed that he thought might someday be useful. And thus equipped, Nico began his travels as a juggler.

Wherever he went, he won praise and silver coins, both of which he stuffed in his pockets. And everywhere he went, there were new tasks that people found to use his skills.

Fire, as it happened, was Nico's greatest accomplishment and ultimately, his undoing. One autumn after a very hot and dry summer, a spark from the campfire of a careless traveler ignited the tinder-dry forest, and a wildfire ensued. The village Nico was staying in that day was directly in the path of the raging fire. The villagers packed everything they could into little carts and fled toward the river, where they were soon trapped by the oncoming flames.

Nico soaked everything he could find in the village well, gathered it all between the raging fire and the dry thatch roofs of the village, and waited.

The fire came with a vengeance.

The first spark that flew toward the houses, Nico snapped out with a damp piece of string. The second larger spark was stopped with a thimble of water. In moments, Nico was splashing water, damp rags, buckets, and wet rocks at the encroaching flames.

The people of the village huddled with their remaining possessions at the edge of the river, watching in amazement. Nico raced from side to side, at war with the flames as only a juggler could be. It seemed almost as though he danced with the fire. There was a rhythm and beauty that emerged from his fierce battle and wherever he flew, the flames died.

Nico drew everything from his pockets and fought the flames with scrambled eggs and pints of cream. He collected sparks on the end of his juggling sticks and doused them in a bucket. He smothered them with rocks and sand. He led them away with string. As the fire towered over him, Nico seemed to shrink in size. Indeed, when all else was consumed, Nico fought the last embers with the sweat from his brow and chased the dying fire back away from the village.

When the smoke cleared, the village was safe. The people returned to their homes in awe that there was no more than a singed roof to count as damage from the fire. But of Nico, there was not a trace. As they gathered the remnants of the battle, they found pieces of string, rocks, and singed sticks. They even found an omelet, a fully baked apple pie, and a crème brûlée. And last of all, they found the juggler's vest—the very one I wear now.

There are those who say that they have seen the juggler wandering yet through forest or dale, and that he juggles great balls of fire to this day, keeping the flames at bay.

19
Gravedigger

BY THE TIME Steven had finished his story, he was standing on one leg on top of a chair, juggling three balls, a stone on the end of a leather thong, and a small shirt-shaped flag. Cherissé was mesmerized by the sight and sat staring at the objects floating in the air with her mouth agape. Steven stepped off the chair while still juggling the odd assortment and approached Cherissé.

"Sleep, Cherissé," he said calmly. Her eyelids fluttered closed and shortly there was a long and loud snore. Steven stared in amazement at the sleeping figure that no longer looked so beautiful, nor young, nor capable. Now he could see the missing teeth, the wrinkles around her eyes, and the long hooked nose. How had he thought this hag was so precious? *It must have been the hit on the head I took,* he thought. He quietly gathered his belongings and slipped out the door.

Steven was nearly to the gate of the hag's house which now looked forlorn and rundown, when he heard the soft honking of the geese. Something had bothered Steven about the docile flock of geese as he stood outside the pen watching the woman feed them and call them by name. The combination of their honks all together sounded almost like voices. He was loath to take away the old woman's livelihood if such they were, but he could not go without opening their pen.

One by one the geese filed out of the pen and as they crossed the threshold, each stood up in the form of a man. Finally, there were seven men standing with Steven.

"Thank you, lad," said the eldest. "The hag laid an enchantment on us and we were kept as geese until she had need of one for the soup pot." Steven gagged as he thought of the goose stew he had eaten with the beautiful young woman when he first woke up. He saw one last goose remaining in the pen.

"Why doesn't he come out?" Steven asked.

"Oh," said the man. "That one's just a goose."

Together the eight men silently left the hag's yard and fled into the woods.

There was some dispute regarding which way they should go, and further dispute regarding whether they should go back and kill the hag. No one seemed anxious, however, to enter her grounds again. Steven sighted the moon and took off walking in what he assumed was a northerly direction. The other men fell in behind him in single file and they walked on through the night.

The men who had been geese became progressively more talkative as the night wore on and they felt they were farther and farther from the hag's clutches. As they walked, they talked—first one at a time, then all at once—of their adventures.

"I ran away from home," said the youngest. "I thought I knew the way to my grandmam's house, but I got lost along the way. As I wandered, weeping in the woods, I came upon a cottage so nicely kept, with a kind motherly woman who dried my eyes and brought me into her house to feed me. Her voice was so soft and comforting and the food so delicious that I thought I would just stay with her a while. Before long, she had me working like a slave to fetch her water, fix her roof, tend her garden. Then one day she sent me to feed the geese. As soon as I entered the pen, she slammed the door shut on me and said, 'You've been a silly goose, now live like one,' and there I stayed until you let me out." The men generally agreed with the boy, but another spoke up.

"It was no kind motherly sort that captured my heart," he said. He wore a rugged black beard and looked like he had been a burly man before he had been forced to eat a diet of grain and scraps. "I was sailing on the sea some leagues away when I heard a sweet and melodious voice singing over the water. I was not heedful of my craft and steered her toward the voice. Before long I was wrecked upon the rocks and near drowned. A nymph with honey hair saved me from the sea and nursed me back to health. I thought I'd never heard a lovelier voice. But from there, my story is the same as the lad's. I worked and slaved for her, just to hear the sound of her voice. Then one day, she sent me to feed the geese, closed the gate on me and told me I'd been a silly goose, now I could live like one. I've been there ever since."

"Aye." "That's right." "I hear you," chorused the other men.

"The lady was not blonde that enticed me away from the road," said a man dressed as a merchant. "I was riding in my cart on a mission of trade from one village to the next. I saw a raven-haired gypsy girl pulling her own little cart. It was stuck in the mud and I offered to help her, thinking we might find something to trade. She said she'd been separated from her caravan and asked so sweetly if I would help her get her cart to the camp. Once we found the wagon where she had camped, she made me a savory stew and sang and danced so sweetly that I completely forgot about my business. She started by getting me to mend a wheel, paint her cart, and finally she showed me a pen of geese and asked me to feed them. When she locked the gate on me she said I was a silly goose and I should live with them. There I was the night you set us free."

One man had been a wood-cutter, one a drunk, and one a soldier. Each had come upon a golden-haired, or red headed, or brown-haired beauty who had a voice so sweet they would do anything to hear her speak again. They had labored for her a short while and then when she said to feed the geese, she'd locked them in her pen.

"I confess," said the geezer, "I was a fool. I am old and my family is poor. I thought to myself that I would no longer be a burden to them and late one night while the family slept, I walked off into the woods thinking to find a quiet place to lie down and die. I found such a place and when I was near to death, I heard an angel singing, calling me up out of my deathbed to join her in the heavens. She gave me a simple place and built my strength with an elixir. She had me do no work at all until the day she asked me to feed the geese for her. I walked into the pen and found myself as silly a goose as I had been." The men all nodded.

"Now, our rescuer," said the geezer. "How did you come to be in her clutches?" Steven told the story of being knocked off the boat and caught in the current, then rescued from her nets, according to the story that Cherissé had told him.

"But how did you get free of her seduction?" asked the geezer.

"Well," said Steven, "we agreed to tell each other stories and when I had finished mine, she had fallen asleep.

In sleep, I could see her for what she was. She was not the most beautiful creature I had ever seen, but the ugliest. And to hear her snore was a sure antidote to her sweet voice. When I left, I was moved to open the pen and let you out."

"She fell asleep when you told a story, eh?" said the geezer.

"Yes," said Steven. He did not bother to tell about the juggling balls that seemed to so captivate her.

"Must not be a very good storyteller," the geezer snorted, and the men all laughed. The sound was almost like the honking of the geese they had been.

By mid-day, the company came to a road and sat to eat some of the scraps that Steven still had in his pack. They had been a little waterlogged and then dried in front of the fire, but no one complained. As they sat, they talked about the direction in which they thought Rich Reach might lie.

At last, amidst a rising squabble, Steven looked at the men, remembered what Cherissé had said about the number of silly geese one meets along the road, and announced that he was going to the right. The old geezer then spoke to Steven.

"You figure that is the way to Rich Reach?" he asked.

"It is the road I will take to get there," answered Steven. The geezer nodded sagely.

"Well, farewell, then," he said. "We don't want to go anywhere near that place. It's haunted." And with that the seven men who had been geese set off the opposite direction along the road.

Steven was relieved, as he picked up his pack and headed in his chosen direction.

THE AFTERNOON PASSED in eerie silence after the blatting of the geese men. Steven trudged along the road he had chosen. He passed no one and there were few dwellings, all of which seemed abandoned and lifeless. He spent the night in the shelter of one and hurried on in the morning. Near midday, Steven saw a tiny leather flag in the shape of a shirt on a post. He wondered if he was entering or leaving the Kingdom of Arining.

About mid-afternoon, he came to a town larger than the abandoned hamlets he had ventured through thus far. There was a low stone arch marking the entry to the town and two or three stone buildings among the timber houses. But there was no one on the street of the town. Steven called out a "Halloo!" that echoed feebly down the empty street.

The well still worked and the water was sweet. There was stale bread still in the bakery, and dried meats at the butcher. There being no one in the town to ask, Steven helped himself to what little food and drink he needed to make a meal and restock his traveling pack. He left a silver coin at each place that he took bread, meat, or wine. Having replenished his rations, he proceeded to head out of the town and continued on his way.

Just as he passed under the arch that marked the boundary of the city, Steven heard whistling. It was faint at first, but stronger as Steven looked up the hill outside the town gate. It was an almost tuneless melody that came from the town's bone yard, where generations of the dead had been buried. Steven wound his way through the stone monuments with names of people on them until he saw a shovel full of dirt come flying from a hole. A head merged shortly thereafter. The head was attached to a rather dirty and scruffily bearded man who whistled as he held a gold chain up to the light.

"Hello?" said Steven, a little uncertainly.

The scruffy man was momentarily startled and quickly thrust the gold chain into his pocket. He turned to Steven and smiled a broad gap-toothed grin.

"Hello there, stranger," said the man. "What brings you to the former Town of Mallowrock?" The man seemed quite friendly and Steven gladly answered.

"I'm Steven George the Dragonslayer," he said. "I'm on a quest to find the Terror of Rich Reach."

"Well, that's a mouthful," said the man. "I'm Tom Jak the Gravedigger, on a quest to fill my pockets with gold."

"Where is the dead man you will be burying?" Steven asked, looking around.

"Oh, he's right here under my feet in this grave."

"You mean you've uncovered him?" asked Steven perplexed.

"Now how else would I find the gold chains and watches, rings and jewels that they buried with him?" asked Tom. "Terrible wasteful of folks to bury all that stuff with the dead. Hundred years later, the body is gone, but the gold is still there."

"So, you aren't really a grave*digger*," said Steven. "You are really more of a grave*robber*."

"I ask you, sir," said Tom Jak, "what is this I'm standing in?"

"A grave," said Steven.

"And what have I been doing with this here shovel all afternoon?" asked Tom.

"Digging?" Steven suggested tentatively.

"A grave and digging. Grave. Dig. Gravedigger," said Tom with finality.

"But you are taking from the grave, not putting people in it," Steven countered. "Grave. Rob. Graverobber."

"No, no, no," said Tom. "You could say maybe grave-taker if you had to. But that makes it sound like I'm taking the grave from one place to another. If I pluck an apple from a tree and eat it, I'm not a tree-robber. And if I fish a trout from the stream, I'm no stream-robber. And no more than if I dig a grave and find a fancy gold chain am I a graverobber. It don't belong to nobody, so now it is mine!"

"But it belonged to the person in the grave," said Steven.

"He's dead!" exclaimed Tom. "I ask you, if a farmer dies, does he own the crops in the field? Does he still own his house? Is his widow still married? No, no, and no. Why? Because the man is dead and dead is dead. It's like saying the grass is owned by the soil, for I'll tell you, this old fellow in this grave is nothing but soil now."

Steven was amazed by the man's logic. He could actually see that it made sense in its own crooked way.

"Don't the people who live here object?" asked Steven.

"The people who live here are all dead," said Tom.

"Everyone in the town died?" exclaimed Steven.

"No. Most of them left," answered Tom. "Just the only ones who are still here are dead. Except me, of course," he amended.

"Why did they leave?" asked Steven.

"The Terror," said Tom in his spookiest voice. "Give me a hand out this grave now, would you? It's time to fill 'er back in." Steven proffered his hand to the gravedigger and Tom climbed out. He took a long pull on a wine jug that lay nearby, and then began filling the hole back in.

"Aren't you afraid of the Terror, too?" asked Steven.

"Ahh, no," said Tom. "It won't bother me. See, the nature of these terror things is to get groups of people to panic and run away. If you don't got a group, you don't got a terror. It's too much work for it to work one person into a panic."

"Did you ever actually see the Terror?" asked Steven.

"No," said Tom. "Can't say I did. In fact, can't say anybody did. Probably wouldn't have scared them so much if they'd seen it. Some said it was an animal. Some said it was a man. Some said it was the dead come back to life. Every time they talked about it, it was bigger and scarier and people got more and more worked up. Then one day, they all up and left in a hurry."

"Where did they go?" asked Steven.

"This way, that way, every way," said Tom.

"Didn't anyone try to find the Terror and stop it?"

"You ask a lot of questions," said Tom, panting with another shovelful of dirt. "Now, I tell you what. You start shoveling and I'll sit here and tell you a story."

"Shall we trade Once Upon a Times?" asked Steven.

"Aye, we shall," said Tom. "I'll tell a story while you shovel, and you can tell a story when we've eaten our fill and drunk at the inn. And tomorrow we'll look at the sun and laugh at the terror again."

And so, Steven began to shovel.

20
The Last Pilgrim

ONCE UPON A TIME, not so long ago, right here in the Town of Mallowrock, there were seven people sitting in the Inn of the Shorn Sheep discussing the increasing presence of the Terror. None of them knew what the Terror was, for none had ever seen it, but these were fine upright citizens who believed that something must be done to stop the Terror.

Now their real names will not interest you, but I will tell you the names I have given them. At the head of the table sat Governor Authority, a watchful man who liked a well-run town. Taxes were paid on time, children went to bed when they were told, and punishment was meted out to those who defied Authority. To the Governor's left, was the long-married couple, Sir Passion and Lady Love. As long as they had each other, both got along well with Governor Authority, but when found alone, they were as likely to flout Authority as to obey him. To the Governor's right was Sergeant Bravery. He was decorated with medals from the wars he had fought and the kings he had served, and there was no one on whom Authority depended more than Sergeant Bravery.

Also at the table was a boy named Youth and a maiden named Beauty. Maid Beauty caught everyone's eye. She had the blush of dawn and was in the blossom of her womanhood. She believed that everything should be blessed by Beauty and often meddled in the keeping of other people's homes and the cleaning of the streets. Next to her, Master Youth was an impetuous fellow, who faced the future squarely and was often harshly critical of where Authority had led them thus far. The future, he declared, belonged to him and Authority should pay more heed.

Finally, there was an old man at the table who called himself Wisdom. It often fell to the old man to arbitrate when there was a disagreement and to counsel both Youth and Authority in their conflicts. It was said all around Mallowrock that everything went better when Wisdom was around.

Now the subject of their gathering on this night, as I said, was the encroaching Terror and what it was doing to the people. All these fine citizens could see that there was a threat and that the denizens of Mallowrock depended on them to find a solution, but they could not agree among themselves what that solution would be. Even Wisdom was at a loss.

Eventually, the old man came up with an idea that seemed good to all of those gathered. There was an oracle at the joining of two rivers in a deep valley, on the other side of the mountains, called the Athenaeum. It was said all answers could be found there.

The seven decided they should travel together to the Athenaeum of Twin Rivers to ask the oracle what they should do about the approaching Terror. They would take whatever advice they received.

So that the people of Mallowrock were not alone and despairing, they decided to leave the beloved Dame Hope in charge of the town while they were absent on their pilgrimage.

Governor Authority ordered a horse and cart to be brought to the door of the Inn and the seven pilgrims set out on their journey. Well, that is to say, they all climbed aboard the cart and took their places, but the cart did not move. Looking for an answer, it was soon discovered there was no one to drive the cart. They called for volunteers to drive them to the Athenaeum of Twin Rivers, and suddenly, the inn yard was silent and empty. No one wanted to undertake this dangerous journey with the seven pilgrims.

It was then that the town's Drunk snored from his resting place on the steps of the inn. Immediately, he was drafted. He was seated on the driver's bench and told to drive the pilgrims out of town and to the Athenaeum of Twin Rivers. You might think this is a strange choice, but there were no other resources to be had and, in truth, Drunk was a good man who just liked his wine a little more than others. After a few tries, he cracked a whip over the horse to pull the cart out of town.

On the right side of the cart were seated Lady Love, Sir Passion, and Old Man Wisdom. On the left side of the cart were Sergeant Bravery, Maid Beauty, and Master Youth. Governor Authority stood in the front of the cart, not, as you might expect, to give direction to the driver, but rather facing the back of the cart so he could better keep an eye on his fellow pilgrims and where they had been.

It was a glorious departure. People from the town turned out to cheer their heroes on and to wish them good speed on their journey. Down the main street of town the cart was pulled, right up to the stone arch at the entrance.

Having driven carts before, when they reached the stone arch, Drunk called out in a slurred voice, "Duck!" But there was so much cheering and adoration going on that Authority paid no heed to Drunk. Thus, it happened that when they went through the stone arch, Authority was struck in the back of the head and fell dead off the cart.

You might think this ended the adventure, but the others were determined to fulfill their pilgrimage, and as they had all bent down to see the fallen Authority, they missed being struck by the arch themselves and did not share his fate. Not noticing the lack of Authority, Drunk continued to drive the horse and cart forward.

During the first few days on the road, Sir Passion noticed that Lady Love looked kindly on Sergeant Bravery. She admired his strength and rugged good looks and smiled on him often. This stirred Sir Passion to action. He argued first with Lady Love, but when she smiled at him just as sweetly, he could not vent his anger.

So, he turned on Sergeant Bravery and challenged him. It was nothing to Sergeant Bravery and he encouraged Sir Passion to be calm. But when Sir Passion struck out at Sergeant Bravery, the soldier stood fast and the attack could not overcome him. Moved to rash acts, Sir Passion threw himself at Sergeant Bravery, but overshot his mark and plunged from the cart down the mountainside and was killed.

Now, there were only five pilgrims in the cart, and though saddened by the loss of Passion, Love continued on with the group.

They had progressed far into the mountains when they first noticed that Maid Beauty was fading. The cold mountain air and harsh wind were taking their toll on her. Though she struggled to maintain the appearance of health, indeed she sickened. Her voice became hollow, her hair tangled, and her eyes dim. Maid Beauty withered in her seat and without being noticed by the determined pilgrims, she died and fell from the cart.

And then there were four pilgrims.

You might find it strange, but Sergeant Bravery, Lady Love, Master Youth, and Old Man Wisdom got on well together. They found they had no real need for Authority and rested more soundly without Beauty or Passion. And so, it was a sad day indeed, when the Pilgrims were accosted by brigands on the road.

They surrounded the cart and demanded the pilgrims render up their valuables. Lady Love, Master Youth, and Old Man Wisdom were in the process of removing their jewels—of course, Drunk had nothing of value—when Sergeant Bravery jumped up to withstand the villains. He was outnumbered, but did that matter to him? No, not at all. He was tired and they were fresh, but did that stop Bravery? No, sir! He fought valiantly to save the others without thought for himself.

He matched blow for blow with their swords and for a time it looked as though he would prevail. But even Bravery has its limits and was eventually overwhelmed by the bandits and killed. The victorious villains took their plunder from the other pilgrims the way they originally intended to and left Drunk to drive them where he would.

It was a dark and stormy night as the cart struggled to the top of the pass. It appeared the poor horse would not be able to crest the mountain. Suddenly, struck by a good idea, Master Youth impetuously leapt from the cart and pushed with all his might. His effort won the summit and the cart picked up speed as it headed downhill on the other side. Youth attempted to leap back into the cart, but was caught in the spokes of the wheel and crushed beneath its weight.

Somewhere as they sped down the far side of the mountain, Wisdom failed and died in the night. Morning found only Lady Love and Drunk still remaining of the party who had left Mallowrock.

Now, Lady Love had never liked Drunk's driving, but she kept her peace thinking that with gentleness and kindness, she would eventually be able to change him. Heedless of her pleas, Drunk allowed the cart to careen down the mountain, gaining speed as they went. It was a particularly harrowing ride, and when the cart slid out of control as they rounded a hairpin turn, Lady Love was thrown from the cart and down the mountain to her death. Oblivious to what had happened, Drunk righted the wagon and continued to drive.

Unknown to the others, Councilman Pride had stowed away in the cart, jealous of the honors heaped on the pilgrims. But Pride would not associate with Drunk, so at the first opportunity, he slipped out of the cart and disappeared into the forest.

So, of all the others, only Drunk survived to seek counsel from the Oracle at the Athenaeum of Twin Rivers. But he never returned. So far as I know, Drunk is still sitting in a quiet room of the Athenaeum listening to the Oracle tell tales.

Having lost Authority, Passion, Beauty, Bravery, Youth, Wisdom, Love, and Pride, the people of Mallowrock abandoned Hope and fled from the town, leaving it the deserted shell you see here now.

LATE THAT NIGHT, after they had eaten their fill and drunk more wine than Steven was used to, they sat before the fire and Steven told his story.

<h1 style="text-align:center">21
The Damsel in Distress</h1>

ONCE UPON A TIME, when giants and dragons, unicorns and great winged horses roamed the earth, there was a fair maiden named Isabella Della Legati. Isabella Della Legati was a damsel in distress. She was locked in a high tower and guarded by a wicked witch. The witch had no friends. She never went anywhere. She didn't like anyone. All Isabella Della Legati did was sit by her window and dream of a day when her Prince Charming would ride up on his white charger and rescue her from her tower and her boring life.

Isabella did not know precisely how long she had been captive in the castle. The witch told her she was eighteen summers old, but the witch, of course, would not tell Isabella anything about her *real* mother, or where she really lived. The witch insisted *she* was Isabella's mother. Hah! Isabella was too smart to fall for that line.

Isabella was certain she must be a princess of some wonderful land where the King and Queen had been in mourning for her for eighteen years. She imagined that she had been stolen from her cradle by the witch, who was jealous because the queen had such a beautiful daughter and the witch didn't. Or perhaps it had been a bargain with a fiend that her poor mother had been forced into to save the life of her beloved husband, the king, and to do so, she had to give up her firstborn. Then again, it could have been punishment because her mother had desired lettuce from the witch's garden and the witch demanded her daughter in payment for the stolen greens.

Isabella looked through one of her many books of Once Upon a Time stories to see if there was a kind of lettuce called Isabella. It sounded a bit more like a type of pasta—Isabella noodles.

Oh, even her name was terrible, and she blamed the witch for that as well. Whatever. One day her prince would come and he would trick the old witch and carry off the princess on his white charger. They would return to the kingdom of her real mother and father and be married and live happily ever after.

She sighed and petted the soft fleece cradle liner she'd had since she was a baby. The witch had tried to get it from her on occasion, but Isabella had made such a fuss for so long that the witch no longer tried to take it from her. Isabella imagined that she would carry the sheepskin with her when she was rescued and it would be all the proof of her identity that she needed when she showed it to her true parents, the king and queen.

She supposed she had better get dinner ready and clean the house before the old hag started nagging her again. You would think she was some common servant girl and not the daughter of royalty. She gave her hair one more brush stroke, wrapped it up on her head, and tied it there with a ribbon. Then she stomped down both cold steps to the kitchen to boil water.

ACTUALLY, ISABELLA HAD very little that she was responsible for in the house. She had to keep her room tidy and help with cooking and dishes. Once a week, she and the witch cleaned the tower thoroughly. Mostly, Isabella sat in her chamber and read the Once Upon a Time stories, or sighed as she stared out the window, waiting for her prince. Sometimes she painted pictures, often very dark, somber pictures that showed the witch in various forms of duress when her prince came to rescue her. She also wrote poetry. Her poems were long rambling verses about the misery of life and how desperate she was to be free.

ISABELLA WAS NOT sure when she first saw the boy out her window. It seemed he stood in the exact same spot some yards distant from the witch's tower, where he was safe. He was partly hidden by a tree, and it was quite by accident that Isabella first saw him. He was tall and thin, a little tousled about his fine red shoulder-length hair. He was dressed in a black sweater and black leather trousers that fit him a little too tightly.

When he glanced up at Isabella, it was with a bit of disdain, as if he had only just noticed her staring at him. Yet, he was there, and Isabella could feel his close-set violet blue eyes on her when she wasn't looking at him. That was when she began sitting more erectly in the window, brushing her long hair repeatedly. There was something mysterious and slightly dangerous about the boy, and Isabella wondered exactly what he was doing there.

On chill nights, the boy would toss a black cloak over his shoulders, mount a dark horse, and ride away from her chamber. Isabella imagined he had just heard of a dangerous beast threatening the neighborhood, or that war had just broken out and he had ridden to His Majesty's aid. Though she never saw him ride, she saw him in the mornings, leaning against his tree as if it were his home.

It did not take long for Isabella to convince herself that this was her savior and that he didn't rescue her right off because he wanted to be sure what obstacles he faced before challenging the old witch.

One day, when Isabella could not stand it any longer, she allowed a scarf to fall from her fingers and flutter to the ground.

She gasped slightly, but loudly enough that the boy looked up at her as the scarf floated to the ground. She stared at it in her most forlorn and desperate way, grasping at her heart as though her most precious possession had just been lost.

The ploy worked. The boy glanced swiftly around to see if he was observed, then took several impossibly long strides and scooped up the scarf from the ground. When he reached her window, Isabella had to reconcile the fact that she was, after all, only a few feet above the ground and could probably have leaned out the window to get her scarf herself. Her tower was really not all that high, considering that the entire witch's house had only two steps in it and was built at the ground's level. When the boy held out her scarf, however, she had to catch her breath as her hand touched his black leather glove and their eyes met.

"You dropped this, milady," he said. His voice was like honey and she gazed into his violet blue eyes.

"Thank you," she whispered. The man bowed his head to her and turned to retreat. Isabella realized she had just promoted him from boy to man when their hands almost touched. She regained her voice and hastened to add, "Who are you?"

He turned back to her. "I am Jean-Isadore Viveneau, at your service, Mademoiselle."

Isabella gasped when she realized he had nearly as many syllables in his name as she did.

"You are my hero," she said dreamily.

"And may I know the name of the damsel I have served?" he asked. This was it for Isabella.

"I am Isabella Della Legati," she said haughtily, and then changed her tone to conspiratorial. "I am a princess held here against my will, waiting for a champion to rescue me."

"Ah, rescuing," said Jean-Isadore knowingly. "Now that is something I know a little about."

"Really?" she asked breathlessly.

"Yes. Just last night I rescued a fat purse from a noble on the road, who held it against its will," he laughed.

Isabella thought this was incredibly heroic. So that was what he did when he rode away at night. He went in search of things to rescue. Isabella was certain now that this must be her Prince Charming, even if he was dressed in black rather than shining armor and rode a black horse instead of a white charger. She could adjust her expectations, she supposed.

"If you rescue me and take me away with you, I am sure the King and Queen will reward you handsomely. As my husband, you would become heir to the throne!" Isabella enthused.

Jean-Isadore cocked an eyebrow at this. Perhaps this was a good idea. The girl was comely and seemed pleasant enough if a little strange to talk to. But if there were truly a throne to be had, her strangeness would be easy to put up with.

"Rescuing takes some planning," he said cautiously. "Do you have proof of your relationship to the King and Queen?"

"Oh, yes," Isabella said dramatically as she pulled the sheepskin to her. "This was my cradle cloth when the witch stole me from my parents. When they see it, they will know exactly who I am and welcome me with open arms."

Well, thought Jean-Isadore, perhaps it was worth a chance. But there were still a few other valuables he wanted to rescue before he left this part of the country, so he quickly devised a plan.

"I don't think I can do it tonight," he said. "But in three days when the moon is dark, I will ride to your window and take you with me to see the King and Queen. Just before that time, you should gather up any coins the witch has in the house, and anything else of value that you can wrap in your cradle cloth—just so we have goods to trade for food on our way to the castle."

"Oh, I will, I will," cried Isabella. "I will gather up her silver needle, the candlesticks, and the coins, and meet you here at the dark of the moon!"

"Do not take these things too soon," said Jean-Isadore, "or the witch will suspect that you are planning to escape. Wait until she has gone to sleep on that night and meet me here at midnight." And with that, Jean-Isadore turned sharply and strode back to the shelter of the grove where his horse waited for the night's adventure.

The next two days were almost unbearable for Isabella. Jean-Isadore did not return to the grove after his night ride and Isabella feared that he had abandoned her after promising to rescue her. The beautiful man of her dreams (less the shining armor and white charger) was out there someplace rescuing someone or something. What if he did not find her worthy of his attention? How could she possibly go on living?

But on the night of the new moon, she waited in her bed until the witch had gone to sleep then quickly ran through the house gathering up coins and silver wherever she could find them. She brought these to her room and wrapped them with her clothes tightly in her sheepskin, tied it with ribbon, and then sat by the window to wait.

Waiting takes a long time. She was certain it was after midnight. She was certain that he had forgotten her. Tears slipped silently from her eyes and she squeezed them shut. As they closed, she drifted off to sleep, dreaming of her knight in shining armor.

She jolted awake to a soft touch on her hand. She looked to see the black horse nuzzling it. Looking up, she saw the burning eyes of her true love behind the slits of a mask. Without a word, he held his hands out to her and she jumped from the window seat into his arms. He snatched the rolled-up sheepskin from the windowsill and at once they were off at a gallop. She saw the witch's tower disappear behind her. It no longer looked so tall nor so threatening, as she rode away into the dark night.

Before dawn fully broke, they arrived at an abandoned farmhouse and went into the barn. Jean-Isadore closed all the doors and shuttered the windows as Isabella fell exhausted onto a pile of hay. When the horse was taken care of, Jean-Isadore came to Isabella, and the two fell together as one.

Isabella awoke as the last rays of the sun were filtering through shutters that had been thrown open by Jean-Isadore. The rescuer was dressed and his horse stood saddled and ready to ride. Isabella stretched out her arms to welcome her lover, but he showed no interest.

"Come," he said. "We must ride in the darkness of night until we are well clear of this province. I have rescued a pony for you to ride."

Isabella was disappointed that she would not spend the night riding in front of him on his black stallion. She just wanted to be in his arms again. But she obeyed and speedily dressed so she was prepared to ride.

"Why do we have to ride at night?" she asked plaintively.

"You don't want the witch to catch you, do you?" asked Jean-Isadore quietly.

"Oh, no!" gasped Isabella. She packed her little bedroll and Jean-Isadore helped her mount the pony. They rode all night again and in the morning, Jean-Isadore found a campsite and built a small fire. He went off into the woods a little way and came back shortly with a squirrel.

"Here," he said, tossing it at Isabella's feet. "Make dinner. I'll go scout the area to make sure we are secure."

"But how am I to make dinner out of a squirrel?" Isabella cried.

Jean-Isadore heaved a great, put-upon sigh. He pulled out his knife and quickly skinned and gutted the squirrel.

"Now," he said. "Put it on a stick and hold it over the fire. I'll be back shortly." He led his horse with him from the circle.

Isabella did as she had been instructed. At the witch's house, she had sometimes made soup in a kettle on the stove, but when the witch had suggested she try to cook other things, she haughtily turned her back.

Now she found that cooking a squirrel on a stick was nothing at all like cooking soup. The fire was hot, but when she got a longer stick, it drooped and the squirrel got ashes on it. She had to be close enough to hold the spit over the fire without getting it in the ashes.

Just after she managed to find a place behind a rock where only her fingers were being singed by the fire, the wind shifted and smoke blew in her face. She thought she would die before the squirrel was cooked enough to eat, or before Jean-Isadore came back.

Eventually, he did come back, made an inspection of the squirrel, and pronounced it edible. Then he pulled a bottle of wine from his cloak.

"I rescued a bottle from an inn not far from here," he said, taking a long swallow and offering it to Isabella. She took a dainty sip and he snatched it back.

"If there is an inn nearby," said Isabella, "why are we camped out here instead of staying there?"

"Well, Princess," said Jean-Isadore, "I am known to that innkeeper, and we do not much like each other. So, I avoid anything more than the quick rescue of a bottle of his finest. We will be much nearer the civilized lands of the King tomorrow. The day after, we may ride by daylight and sleep in an inn at night." He licked his fingers after picking the squirrel carcass clean and pulled Isabella to him. "Come here, my beauty, and warm my cold night."

"It's daylight," Isabella said, pouting.

"So it is," Jean-Isadore said and yawned. "We'd better get to sleep."

The next night was much a repeat of the previous, but shorter. Jean-Isadore found a haymow they could sleep in. At last, they fell together and all Isabella's fears were put to rest in the arms of her lover.

They traveled by day the next day, and stayed in an inn at night. Jean-Isadore spent some of Isabella's coins for the room and meal and then took her to bed again. By this time, however, Isabella had lost all joy in the routine coupling after which Jean-Isadore fell rapidly asleep.

IN A FEW days' time, the couple reached the castle of the King. Jean-Isadore called a guard to him and asked directions for an audience with the King. The guard called a chamberlain and Jean-Isadore proudly declared, "I bring the Princess Isabella to be reunited with the King and Queen, for long they have been parted."

The chamberlain was puzzled by this, but took the message to the royal court. Intrigued by the curious declaration, The King and Queen granted audience to Jean-Isadore and Isabella.

When they arrived in the royal court, it was not quite what either had expected. King Alphonse and Queen Antonia were not much older than Isabella. When Isabella made her case and laid the sheepskin at their feet, the King and Queen were even more puzzled. No, there was no missing princess of any age. No, King Alphonse was the sole heir to the throne and had never had a sister. Isabella was heart-broken.

"We must have the wrong king and queen," she said at last.

Jean-Isadore heaved a sigh of resignation and turned to leave. Just at that time a courtier spoke up.

"Wait a minute!" He declared. "This is the highwayman that robbed me not a fortnight ago! Arrest this man!" Everyone was taken aback and the highwayman, Jean-Isadore Viveneau, blanched.

"That can't be!" Isabella said. "He is a prince and rescued me from an evil witch!"

"A prince of thieves, perhaps," said the courtier. Guards came forward to arrest Jean-Isadore. The highwayman gave a small shrug of his shoulders and a weak smile at Isabella, then dove out a window. Isabella and the guards rushed to the window to look in time to see Jean Isadore pull himself out of the moat, whistle for his horse, and ride away. Isabella collapsed by the window weeping.

THE KING AND Queen were merciful, but not willing to let Isabella off for what they determined was her charade. She was put to work in the kitchens, where she learned very well how to prepare a great many dishes, and after seven years, she had earned freedom for herself and her young son. She took him and booked passage back to her small village, where a very old woman met her at the door that had once been such a barrier to Isabella's freedom.

She pled with the old woman for forgiveness and begged to be taken back in.

When people asked the old woman why she would ever take back the foolish girl and her illegitimate brat, the old woman's answer was always the same.

"She is my daughter and he is my grandson. What else would I do?"

Isabella lovingly cared for the old woman until the day her mother died, and never referred to her as a witch again. Nor did she wait to be rescued. The highwayman was never heard from again in that kingdom, though tales are told of him abroad. And the sheepskin she carried is the very one I was laid on as a child and which I wear as a vest to this day.

22
Grave

TOM THE GRAVEDIGGER and Steven talked companionably well into the night as they drank wine from the supply in the inn. Steven put a silver coin on the bar for each bottle they took. Tom gravely went behind the bar, tapped the coin twice on the wood, and then pocketed it. Steven laughed at the gravedigger until tears ran from his eyes.

In the morning, Steven was awakened from where he had fallen asleep next to the fire by joyful whistling outside the inn. He staggered to his feet, holding his head. He was not used to sharing such a large quantity of wine and his head threatened to explode with every step.

The whistling proved to be coming from the gravedigger as he scuffled around outside, preparing his tools for another day in the cemetery. He greeted Steven cheerfully and pushed a cup of hot steamy liquid into his hands.

"Drink this," Tom said, brightly. "You'll have your head back in no time."

Steven dutifully sampled the liquid and found that it was surprisingly bitter and pleasant all at once. He burnt his tongue on the first sip, but was progressively able to take more of the liquid down. His stomach began to settle and his headache diminished.

"Are you going back to dig more graves?" Steven asked.

"Yes," said Tom, solemnly. "A man's work is never done. I figure I have three more days of safely liberating the treasures of yon graveyard before I need to pick myself up and move far away."

"Why only three days?" Steven asked. "Surely no one is coming back here while the Terror is terrorizing them."

"That's just it," Tom said, forlornly. "The Terror will be gone in that time, so the people will start returning. They aren't likely to notice that the ground has been turned for the first few days they are back, but if there were open holes, they'd get suspicious mighty fast. It wouldn't be healthy for me to actually be digging graves when they arrived."

"Why do you think they will start returning in three days?" asked Steven.

"Well now," said the gravedigger, "where did you say you were heading to?"

"Rich Reach," Steven answered.

"That would be about three days' journey from here," Tom said. "Which means that when people see you and hear that you've vanquished the Terror, they'll give you a hero's welcome and then head back home. By the time they get three days back here, I want to be three days in that direction." Tom pointed off the way from which Steven had approached the village.

Steven chewed on some dry bread and shouldered his pack as the two walked back out toward the cemetery. Tom was an odd man who had his own sense of right and wrong, but Steven had found his company to be pleasant and entertaining.

"I hope we will meet again, Tom Jak the Gravedigger," Steven said. "You would be pleasant company on the road."

"I would come with you now if it weren't for the work," Tom answered. "It would certainly please me if our paths crossed again."

They came to the graveyard and Tom motioned Steven on in.

"There is something else I wish to show you, Master Dragonslayer," Tom said. "It is a secret that will stead you well when you go to conquer the Terror." They walked to the far side of the bone yard where there was an open grave already dug. There was no stone near this grave, however.

"Whose grave is this?" Steven asked.

"It is mine," said the gravedigger. Steven was startled and stared at Tom.

"Do you mean to say you are dead?" Steven asked, horrified.

"You aren't really very smart, are you?" Tom sighed. "Do I look dead to you? No. I'm very much alive and plan to stay that way for as long as I can. But life is a road that goes ever downhill. You are born in the morning and are dead by dinner. By breakfast the next day, you are nothing but dirt in the field. The living die, but the dead never live."

"But you said this was your grave," Steven protested.

"And my grave it is, if I should die where I stand. You could just roll me in and cover me up," Tom said. "However, if you were to do that, all the silver coins are in a pouch around my neck, and the gold and jewels I've found are in my pack. Don't be foolish and bury it all."

"Are you planning to die now?" Steven asked.

"Oh no!" exclaimed Tom.

"Then why have you dug your grave?"

"To look into it," said Tom suddenly serious. "You cannot look into your own grave and ever know a greater terror."

Tom stood and stared down into the hole. Steven came up beside him and stared down into the hole as well. Tom looked up.

"Doesn't do you any good to look into my grave," Tom said. "Yours is over there." He pointed and a few yards away Steven saw another open grave. "Thought you might need it," Tom said pleasantly.

Steven looked at the gravedigger and cautiously crossed to the open grave and looked over the edge.

Steven had known all his life that he was born to master a dragon, but it had been a much different experience than he expected. Dragons, after all, never truly have a master. But Steven had embarked on that adventure knowing it was likely he would die. Then, after seven years of traveling with Madame Selah Welinska, he had grown comfortable in the thought of growing old with the dragon-lady.

Then the summons from the king had come and Selah had… vanished. Steven was feeling particularly mortal. He had nearly been killed by a bear. He had met a king. He had journeyed to where a witch attempted to enchant him. He had shared stories with a gravedigger, and now he was at the edge of his grave.

He did not know what grisly death would bring him to this hole in the ground. What was the Terror of Rich Reach? What would it do to Steven when they met? Steven wanted nothing more than to turn and run back the way he had come. Even living as a goose with the enchantress would be better than this unknown fate.

He took a deep breath and stared down into the pit. He stood there for some time. He didn't know what he expected to see, but it wasn't this. At last, he tore himself away from the grave and looked at Tom, still standing by his own grave, grinning from ear to ear.

"It's just a hole," Steven called over to Tom.

"Well now," Tom said. "You've suddenly gotten wisdom. What else is it you have to fear?"

Steven began to laugh. It hurt his head a little, but he could not restrain himself. Tom tossed Steven a shovel and the two began to fill in their respective graves. When they were finished, Steven embraced Tom and returned to the road. His last sight of the gravedigger was of the man digging into the dirt in front of an opulent headstone. He could hear Tom's happy whistle long after he had lost sight of the man.

IT WAS LATE afternoon when Steven approached a crossroads and decided it was a good place to camp. For the first time since he had left the road at the Town of Tornlace, he saw a marker pointing the way to Rich Reach. He snared a rabbit for dinner and built a fire to cook it over. It was not yet dusk when he heard a tumult coming from one of the crossroads.

Coming toward him, Steven saw a ragtag band of travelers pushing and pulling carts, pigs, sheep, and two oxen. The carts were filled to overflowing with goods and the people seemed in near panic. Bouncing around them was a small man in a black cassock, exhorting them to hurry.

"We must make camp before dark at the crossroads," the man said as he helped push a wagon across the road, "before it comes."

Steven rose to help the strangers.

"Please, come and join my camp," Steven said. "I have a fire ready and more than I can eat."

The travelers were startled to see Steven suddenly appear, but the monk encouraged them on.

"Splendid! Splendid!" he cried. "Our savior. There is safety in numbers. Stay together. Don't stray from the fire!"

The people pushed their carts into a rough circle around Steven's campfire and the two dozen travelers hastened to create an encampment inside the circle. Several brought more wood to build the fire up and additional food supplies began to appear.

"Why do you travel so hurriedly?" Steven asked.

"Do you not know of the Terror?" the monk asked. "It is right behind us, bringing terrible things in its wake. We must seek safety in Rich Reach."

The other travelers seemed too frightened to engage in conversation.

"Who are you?" demanded the monk.

"I am Steven George the Dragonslayer. It is because of the Terror that I have come to the Principality of Rich Reach," Steven spoke as he smiled at the people.

"Ah, Steven George the Storyteller, as I've heard it said," answered the monk. "I am Cleophas, holy monk and shepherd of my people. We are traveling to Rich Reach for safety. Then I will return to fetch more, to spread word of the Terror and to encourage people to flee."

When the monk spoke, the people all seemed hypnotized by his voice. He captured the ear, and if Steven had not recently experienced the subtle charm of Cherissé, he, too, might have fallen under its spell.

"Well, there is no terror here," he said confidently. "I doubt that there is a terror anywhere," he concluded.

"A storyteller tells us there is no fear," mocked the monk. "A dragonslayer who mastered his dragon with words. Where is your dragon now, Master Dragonslayer?" asked the monk.

Steven was puzzled at how the monk knew so much about him. It seemed he was set to ridicule Steven in front of these people.

"How do you know me, sir?" asked Steven.

"Your stories go before you, Dragonslayer," the monk answered. "I know all about your journeys and how you trick people with your lies. You tell them one thing and then go on your way without caring what your story has done to them."

"I do not tell lies," protested Steven George. "I tell stories."

"Your stories are not true," said Cleophas. "I can tell stories that are true, and they will shake the skin from your bones. For I have seen the Terror, and it is coming for us all."

"Do tell," said Steven, settling onto his bedroll to wait. "We shall Once Upon a Time each other and let these poor refugees decide what is true." The monk stood to tell his story.

23
The Gathering Storm

ONCE UPON A TIME, in the days that true heroes walked the earth, the world was ruled by four great chieftains. Athriel the Fair ruled the Nation of the East. He seemed slight and very unlike a hero, but he was swift. He could rush in upon his enemies before they knew what was about to happen. Like the wind, he was swift and sure and seemed to be everywhere at once.

Hotheaded Skoldor ruled all the Nation of the South. He had flaming red hair and rose to anger at the smallest provocation. His anger consumed everything in its path. Even his own soldiers learned to follow safely behind Skoldor so they would not be in his fiery path.

Easy-going Rael held the Nation of the West. His flowing golden locks sat easily above the deep blue eyes that could pierce into the very soul. It was hard to know the exact boundaries of the Nation of the West because they seemed to ebb and flow with the tides of the great sea on which it bordered.

Finally, there was dark and brooding Borion who ruled the Nation of the North. Some say his face was carved of rock, for his expression never wavered. His eyes were the same in laughter as in weeping. It was, it is said, impossible to know what he thought or when he might strike.

With four such powerful chieftains, you might expect that there was conflict, and, indeed, their borders were never quiet. Borion responded to Rael's shifting borders with hardened lines of defense. The suddenness of Athriel's presence fanned the ardor of Skoldor and conflict raged. But all these great heroes paid common fealty to the one Lord greater than all: Chrivu the Mighty.

Chrivu had no nation, no army, and no allegiance. Chrivu rode where he pleased and slept wherever he lay his head. Each of the four great chieftains had at one time or another challenged Chrivu for the right to rule all, but each had failed and barely escaped with his life.

Chrivu had disdain for all, for no one was as mighty as Chrivu. He drank the sea and pissed the rivers. He walked through fire as though it were nothing. When the wind blew in his face, he sucked it into his lungs until the wind was exhausted. And when a mountain rose before him, he flattened it with his fist rather than walk around. Never before and never since has there been a hero like Chrivu.

If there was a dispute between the rival chieftains, Chrivu might show up on either side of the conflict and subdue the other. The balance of the rivalries might be shifted at any moment by Chrivu's word. After the chieftains had suffered the uncertainty for a hundred years, they came together in treaty to talk.

"We must conquer Chrivu," said Athriel. "He diminishes our prowess and respect among our people."

"Indeed," Boriel answered. "The people believe he is their king and not we."

"None of our borders are safe as long as he lives," said Rael.

"But how shall we bring him down?" fumed Skoldor.

The chieftains shook their heads and then as one uttered a single word.

"Oawo!"

Oawo was an ancient wise woman who lived alone in the mountains. It was said that she was present at the birth of the ocean and was midwife to the desert. She was so ancient that when she was asked a question, it sometimes took days before her jaw hinge became unstuck so she could answer. But the wisdom she imparted never failed.

It was also rumored that she was Chrivu's mother, imprisoned in the mountain so she would never challenge him. It was to her that the chieftains took their suit.

The old woman pried her eyes open to look at them through the gloom of the cavern. Then her shaking hand withdrew a silver strand of her hair that had not been cut in two hundred years and held it out to them.

"You must act as one in order to master Chrivu," she croaked. "He cannot be bound as other men can, but by the hair of his mother's head. You must take this and wrap it tightly around him. This will immobilize him. Then you can take his head. But beware. If he is free of this strand, he will regain his head and come back stronger than before and more terrible as well. Do not let him free, even after he is dead."

With that, she fell silent again. The great chieftains took the strand of Oawo's hair and left the cavern in secret.

On the appointed day, the four lay in ambush as Chrivu came from the forest toting a deer he had killed for dinner. They waited until Chrivu had gorged himself on the venison and fell asleep, then they leapt to capture him. Chrivu jumped up, grabbing his great battle axe to swing at the head of the nearest chieftain, but Skoldor blocked the blow with his hammer while Rael rushed him with his sword. While Chrivu was occupied battling the two heroes, Boriel anchored the thread of hair around Chrivu's feet and swift Athriel rushed around the great Lord winding the thread around his legs, arms, and shoulders. At last, great Chrivu's axe fell at his feet and he could no longer move.

Triumphantly, Boriel raised Chrivu's axe and severed his head. They mounted the head on a pole which became the face in the mountains that so many have seen in the centuries since. The four chieftains dug a deep pit in which to cast the body, but before they did, Rael made a suggestion.

"Well I remember the words of the old lady Oawo," he said. "I would not have Chrivu rise from the grave and regain his head. Let us, therefore, sever his hands and his feet so that if he should come to life, he can do no harm for he will be unable to do battle or to march to war."

This seemed right to the chieftains who swiftly carried out the bloody sentence and buried the remainder of the body in the pit. The four agreed each to take one of the severed hands and feet to the furthest reach of his nation and bury it so that it could never be reunited with Chrivu's body.

And that was the death of Chrivu.

It is said that Athriel was slain first. A hand came from nowhere and strangled him as he slept. Hot-tempered Skoldor was trampled beneath the feet of a stampede of horses, but it was a human footprint that marked his head. Rael saw a hand swing a sword, but never saw who wielded it as he fell dead. And Boriel, as he looked over his nation from a high cliff, was suddenly kicked over its edge by a foot that came from nowhere.

Since that day, the severed hands and feet of Chrivu have been journeying to rejoin his buried body, for the four heroes failed to keep all the Lord's parts bound by the strand of hair. When they reach the rest of Chrivu's body, they will unbind him and reclaim his head from the mountain, and Chrivu will rise more terrible than ever.

We have seen the Terror coming, but I say to you, we have seen only Chrivu's hand as it journeys to reunite with his body. Whosoever that hand touches will surely die.

ALL WERE SILENT at the telling of the monk's story. They quaked in their bedrolls and edged nearer the fire. Then in the silence a hand dropped, seemingly out of nowhere, and landed on Steven's chest.

"Duck!" screamed the monk. "It has found us. Flee! Flee!" The poor panicked refugees dove for cover and scrambled into the underbrush.

Steven lay on his bedroll with the severed hand on his chest. It was withered, but it also wore a ring on its finger— a ring Steven recognized. He picked up the lifeless hand and flung it toward the fire.

"No!" screamed the monk as he made a diving catch before the appendage hit the flames. "Not in the fire! My hand!" He cradled the fingers in his arms and Steven could see the stump that protruded from the long black sleeve. The monk lay on the ground whimpering and was not nearly as frightening as he had been only moments before. "My hand, my precious hand," the monk continued to whimper.

"Pablo Ibin Ariaga, Thief of Byzantium," Steven called out to the monk. "Come out, come out wherever you are."

The monk jerked upright with a snarl and pulled himself to his feet to face Steven.

"Who are you to summon me, Steven George the Liar," asked the man in the robes of a monk. He threw back the cowl on the habit and Steven could see his face clearly in the firelight. "You lied to me! Now look at me!"

"I have never lied to you," Steven said calmly.

"You said that a hand severed with that sword would reattach itself. I chose the weapon that cut off my right hand and clutched it to myself as I fled the marketplace," Pablo Ibin Ariaga stuttered in his rage. "It never grew together. I held it in place. I lashed it to my wrist with leather straps. I nearly died, but it never grew together. You lied! You lied! You lied!"

"It wasn't a lie," Steven said, indignantly. "It was a story. How can you imagine that a mere story would be a fact? Are there ogres to slay? Gnomes in the garden? Damsels to rescue? Dragons to master? They are stories."

"But my stories are true," cackled the thief. "Just ask the villagers if you can find any left. The Terror stalks them and drives them from their homes. Men have died when the hand has struck them. You should have died!"

"The Terror is just a story," said Steven, "and people have believed it like you believed that the sword could sever your hand and reattach it. What people believe doesn't make it true."

"But you know the Terror is real, Steven George," said Pablo, "else why have you not looked into my eyes? Come my little dragonslayer friend. Come look into my eyes. Are you afraid?"

When Steven had first met the thief so many years ago, he had fallen under his spell when he looked into his eyes. Steven remembered how the deep black wells of Pablo's eyes could mesmerize you. How his voice could turn you into his servant in moments. He also remembered how Pablo had taken everything Steven had—his horse, his knife, his sword, his coins—and left him with only a donkey. Well, that had worked out all right in the end.

Steven slowly raised his eyes to look deeply into Pablo's. They held each other, locked in a gaze as if each awaited the other's first blink. There was no sound but the crackling of the fire. Suddenly Pablo shook his head violently and backed away from Steven.

"What has happened to you, Dragonslayer?" he asked. "Have you indeed mastered your terror?"

"Thief," Steven said, "I have looked into my own grave. What fear should I have of you?"

The thief backed away another step and turned to run. Steven reached into the pocket of his vest and pulled out three hard round balls, which he launched in rapid succession at the back of the fleeing thief. They struck and the thief fell forward. Steven stood over him with a foot in the middle of his back.

"Pablo Barcenas Ibin Ariaga, I arrest you in the name of the King. All those who honor their lands and the kingdom of Montague Magnus, come out and witness the arrest of the Terror of Rich Reach," Steven intoned in a loud voice. The frightened refugees crept out from the shadows slowly.

"By what authority do you arrest me?" the thief cried. "I am a free man. I've paid my debt with my right hand. All I did was tell stories. You have no authority to arrest me."

Steven reached into his pocket again and pulled out a leather thong with a rock at the end. He placed the thong over his neck.

"I arrest you as a member of the King's Guard," he said. "The crime is terrorizing the Principality of Rich Reach."

Again, Steven reached in his pocket. This time, he pulled out a ball of yarn given to him by Orithyia the Spinner. With this, Steven bound Pablo's arms to his sides, being unable to tie his hands together. The spun wool was strong and held the prisoner firmly, as if he were Chrivu awaiting execution. At this, the rest of the refugees emerged from the shadows whispering.

"Is it true?"

"Was this the terror?"

"Is this all?"

"This is all that you were afraid of," Steven said calmly. "You may not believe yet, but the fear was inside you. Now gather round. I owe a story debt to this thief and I will tell it before we sleep."

24
The Pinpoint of Light

ONCE UPON A TIME, long ago and more steps away than I can count, there was a little village near a river but very far from anything else. That village dwelt in darkness. This darkness was not metaphorical, as in ignorance. It was quite literal. The sun never shone. It was dark and cold like midnight under a cloudy sky in the middle of winter. The people huddled together for warmth. They wore sheepskin clothes to keep from freezing. Even their meager fires seemed to give no light or warmth, so complete was the darkness.

When it seemed the village would never see light again and despaired of all hope, the village elder called for Quaidulac the Shaman. Quaidulac had not been a shaman for long in this village. He had been caught sitting by the river's edge some time before, thinking of how he could end his life, because he was so cold and miserable. The people found him there, nearly frozen to death and called him Quaidulac, which means "Dreaming by the Water."

"Quaidulac," said the elder, "we are a people of darkness who dwell in darkness, but we cannot remain like this forever. We call on you to journey to the Kingdom of the Sun and beg of him to visit our little village so that we might have warmth and light. Therefore, take what herbs you need, your sheepskins, and your staff, and undertake this journey on our behalf."

Now, Quaidulac did not know what to do. He had never undertaken a spirit journey. He had simply been too cold to move when the people found him by the river. But he thought that it would be much better to travel to this Kingdom of the Sun the elder spoke of than to stay here in the village and continue to suffer the cold and darkness. So Quaidulac packed a satchel of herbs, donned his warmest sheepskins, picked up his staff, and left the village, vowing that he would return with the Sun and light.

Once away from the village, Quaidulac walked aimlessly in the darkness. He had no sense of direction, following the river when it let him and wandering in the forests when it did not. Wherever he went, it was cold and dark. Then, when it seemed most hopeless and Quaidulac sat dreaming of the Kingdom of the Sun, he saw a pinpoint of light in the distance. It flickered and was gone and then came back again. Quaidulac rose at once to follow this pinpoint of light. It seemed so far away, and often flickered out of his vision, but gradually it became steadier.

Quaidulac followed the light for many hundreds of steps, thinking always that it must get bigger or brighter, but it never seemed to change.

Then Quaidulac ran into a wall. He did not see the wall, so focused was he on the light. When he recovered his senses, Quaidulac realized that he had come to a cottage, and that the light he saw was a candle in the window. He found the door of the cottage and having scratched at the entrance, he pushed it open and said, "Hello."

"Hello, Quaidulac," answered a voice in the darkness. "Come in and sit down. I have been waiting for you."

Quaidulac entered the tiny cottage and sat beside the candle. He could faintly make out the figure of a person on the other side.

"Do you know how to reach the Kingdom of the Sun?" Quaidulac asked his host.

"I do," said the voice. "I am your guide."

"What are you called?" Quaidulac asked.

"I am called Candlemaker. I offer a pinpoint of light to guide the seeker," the voice said. "Now, about your quest. No one ever reaches the Kingdom of the Sun."

Quaidulac was crushed. He was so certain a moment ago that his quest was over.

"But you said…"

"Yes. I will show you how to bring the Kingdom of the Sun to your village," answered Candlemaker. "Kingdom of the Sun goes where it will and where it is wanted. You must call to it if you wish it to come to you."

"And how shall I call?" asked Quaidulac.

"You must gather your village and teach them this chant," Candlemaker answered.

And thus, Quaidulac began his education with Candlemaker. Candlemaker taught Quaidulac the chant and the lore of the Sun King. He told Quaidulac of the Sun King's journey to the far lands and his desire to return home. The Sun King, it seemed to Quaidulac, yearned for his village as much as his village yearned for it.

"But surely, this is too simple," said Quaidulac. "How will I get my people to believe such a simple chant can bring the Sun back?"

"Take this candle back to your village," answered Candlmaker. "Have your people look deeply into its flame when they chant. They will see the Sun King approach."

So, Quaidulac thanked Candlemaker and took the candle and returned to his village.

When Quaidulac gave his people the instructions Candlemaker had given him, they were doubtful, but they gathered around the candle and stared into its flame. Soon they began to chant.

"Kum dada. Kum dada tudé. Kum dada. Kum dada sundé." Over and over they repeated the chant, and as they looked into the flame, the flame grew brighter and in its depths they saw the Sun King returning to the land and daybreak came to the tiny village.

The people were ecstatic. They rose and danced. They chanted and laughed. Day came and chased away the night. And then the days became longer and longer. And soon there was no night.

Now you might think this was a happy ending to the story, but you would be mistaken. Where the people had been cold, now they were hot. They stopped chanting the Sun chant and hid the candle, but the Sun King was comfortable in the village and stayed. The people found it difficult to sleep in the bright light. The water dried up and the people were thirsty and the animals were hungry, as the grass withered in the fields. The people tore the arms off their sheepskin jackets and wore only the vests.

And finally, the elder went to Quaidulac the Shaman and said, "Quaidulac, go to the Moon Queen and beg mercy of her, for all the people will perish in this heat. Take your herbs, your sheepskin, and your staff and undertake this quest for us." And so, Quaidulac took his herbs, his sheepskin, and his staff and set off to find the Moon Queen and beg her to return.

The light was now so bright that Quaidulac could no longer see the shapes of things around him, so he wandered aimlessly, searching for the Moon Queen. At long last, he saw a speck of darkness in the distance. It was there and then it was not there, as if the darkness flickered in the light, then returned.

Quaidulac walked on toward the darkness until he ran into a wall that he could not see and discovered that the pinpoint of darkness was a candle that burned a black flame. He found the door of the cottage, and after he had scratched, he called out.

"Hello? Candlemaker, are you there?"

"Hello, Quaidulac. Come in and sit down. I have been expecting you," said Candlemaker.

So, Quaidulac entered the cottage and sat down next to the black flame. Across from him he could barely make out the shadow of Candlemaker.

"Candlemaker," said Quaidulac, "the Sun King has come to my village and will not leave. The water has dried up, the grass has withered, and the people cannot sleep. I must travel to the Moon Queen and beg her to return to our village, but I do not know how to reach her."

"You cannot reach her," said Candlemaker, and Quaidulac despaired.

"Then we are doomed," said Quaidulac.

"No," said Candlemaker. "You must call her to you as you called the Sun King." And so, Quaidulac underwent his training in the chants of the Moon Queen. When he was ready to return to his village, Candlemaker gave him the candle that burned with a black flame and told him to have the people stare into the darkness and summon the Moon Queen.

When Quaidulac got back to his village, the people all gathered around. They anxiously peered into the dark flame and began to chant Candlemaker's chant.

"Kum mama. Kum mama bak bak. Kum mama. Kum mama tunak."

Over and over they chanted the summons for the Moon Queen to return and soon darkness appeared on the horizon and night fell. The nights grew gradually longer as the Sun King was driven from the village and the Moon Queen smiled on them. But when the nights grew very long and darkness and cold threatened to overwhelm the village, the people hid away the black flame and drew out the white flame. Then they repeated the summons for the Sun King and the days got longer.

And so it has been from that time since. When the winter nights are longest and darkness seems to overwhelm all, the people come together to chant over the white candle.

"Kum dada. Kum dada tudé. Kum dada. Kum dada sundé."

And when the days grow long and hot and the grain is ripening in the fields, the people draw forth the black flame Candlemaker gave them and again they chant.

"Kum mama. Kum mama bak bak. Kum mama. Kum mama tunak."

So the people learned that they could look into both the candle of light and the candle of night, and both were good in their own way.

That village was my village, and this is the sheepskin vest that I wear as a reminder of our humble task.

IN THE MORNING, the refugees triumphantly bound the thief to the topmost cart and marched back the way they had come. The thief, they said, would be kept under close watch in their village until the Prince determined what should be done with him. Steven was content with this for, in truth, he was not looking forward to traveling with the thief. Instead, he set his face back toward Rich Reach. With a light step, the ground, even though uphill, seemed to fly beneath his feet.

25

Boundaries

AS STEVEN NEARED a dense stretch of forest, he heard an argument. It seemed to be coming from just off the road ahead, and while two sides of an issue were being hotly discussed, it sounded like only one voice.

"It's been moved."

"How do you know?"

"It didn't used to be here."

"Where did it used to be?"

"Over there."

"Prove it."

"Can't prove it. I'd have to go over there."

"Ha! So, it hasn't been moved."

"It has been moved."

Steven rounded a bend in the road and saw a man pacing back and forth in front of a small pole with a flag on it. As the man paced back and forth, he continued to argue… with himself.

"Dare you to go over there and show me."

"Can't go over there. Over there is not here."

"Take the marker and move it."

"Can't move it. That's illegal."

"But if someone else moved it…"

"…then they broke the law."

"So, move it back."

"But moving it is illegal."

Steven approached the man cautiously, making a great deal of noise to announce his presence. Eventually, the man looked up and noticed Steven. His posture was defensive until he looked carefully at Steven. Then he suddenly called out.

"Here, you. Come here and help me with this," the man called out.

Steven approached cautiously. The man was armed with a sword, but Steven recognized the uniform of a guard, complete with the leather thong and rock around his neck. He pointed at the pole with a flag on it and commanded, "Look!"

Steven looked.

The guard looked.

Together they looked at the pole for several minutes.

"Well, what do you think?" asked the guard at last.

"What do I think of what?" asked Steven.

"Of the marker pole," answered the guard.

"Well," Steven said brightly, "it seems to be sturdy. And straight. It is a fine pole stuck firmly into the ground." Steven smiled at the guard and raised an eyebrow.

"Has it been moved?" the guard asked.

"I don't know," answered Steven truthfully. "I've never seen it before."

"Ah! Now what do you think of that? There's proof. He's never seen it before. Therefore, it wasn't here. Now it is here, ergo, it has been moved. QED. Quid pro quo. Suma cum die."

"I beg your pardon, sir," Steven began. "Whatever are you asking?"

"I am attempting to prove that this boundary marker, marking the boundary of the Principality of Rich Reach in the Kingdom of Arining, has been moved. The fact that you have never seen it before is proof positive that it was not here." The guard retrieved a tally pad from his uniform and began marking in it the exact location of the errant boundary pole.

"But I have never seen you before, either," said Steven. "I've never been here before." Suddenly the guard looked at Steven suspiciously.

"You are a member of the royal guard as tokened by the rock hanging from your neck," said the guard. "How can you have never seen this boundary pole?"

"I've just come from Mariria to visit Prince Valentine of Rich Reach on behalf of King Montague Magnus," said Steven.

"Really?" said the guard.

"Yes," said Steven.

"Well, that is no help at all then," said the guard. "How am I supposed to show that the boundary marker has been moved now?"

"Where was it before?" asked Steven.

"Over there," said the guard pointing off a few yards.

"Let us go see if there is a hole where the pole was removed over there," suggested Steven.

"You can't do that," said the guard.

"Why not?" asked Steven. The guard looked at Steven as if he were explaining the rising of the sun to a child.

"These flags mark the boundary of the Principality of Rich Reach of the Kingdom of Arining," began the guard. "This side of the boundary flag is Arining. That side is not. If we, two guards of the Kings Court, were to cross to that side, it might be seen as an act of aggression. We would have crossed the frontier into foreign territory."

"What would happen?" asked Steven.

"Why all matter of evil might happen," said the guard. "We might even become one of them," he whispered.

"Who are they?" Steven whispered back.

"Why, the others," said the guard, surprised that Steven could not see what was so obvious.

"What are the others?" persisted Steven.

"Why people like you and me, of course," said the guard.

"So, what is the problem?" asked Steven.

The guard paced back and forth in front of the flag. It appeared that he had begun to argue with himself again, but so far, he was doing it quietly. Finally, Steven decided to take matters into his own hand.

"I will just go over there to check for holes while you discuss the situation," said Steven.

"Oh, you can't do that," said the guard.

"Why not?" Steven asked.

"Because then you would be over there and not over here," answered the guard worriedly.

"Now what is the worst that could happen?" Steven asked. He stuck a foot over the imaginary line. "Will my foot fall off?" He leapt over the line and back again. "Will a war start?" He stepped deliberately across the line and turned to face the guard. "Will my teeth fall out? My nose grow longer? My hair turn green? Will I grow into a giant or shrink to a dwarf? Will my hands grow an extra thumb, or my face an extra eye?"

Now Steven was becoming worked up as he warmed to the idea of being blocked by an imaginary line from traveling wherever he might want.

"I ask you," Steven continued, "why do you need a boundary marker? Will people on one side or the other suddenly speak a different language? Will they not still raise their families, market their goods, and bury their dead? Would the world fall apart if there were no boundary poles? If kings did not know where their lands ended, would they not be forced to be fairer when dealing with all the people? Would they not be more peaceful if they didn't claim to own so much at all?"

Steven plucked the boundary pole out of the ground, much to the guard's consternation, and began parading with it around the guard.

"Is this a magic wand that might turn the grass on one side to grain and the grass on the other side to tares? If I carry the boundary pole around you, are you inside the boundary or outside? If there was no boundary pole here, would people stop traveling the road? Would the rivers cease to know where to flow?"

Steven pulled the tiny leather shirt-flag from the top of the pole and continued to march with the pole.

"Is it the pole that marks the boundary or the flag?" he asked. "Without the flag is the pole anything but a stick of wood? Without the stick of wood is the flag nothing but a tiny leather shirt made for a child's toy? Make all the poles into kindling and all the flags into doll clothes. Would the world not be better off if people were free to live where they will without fear of poaching on their king's land or trampling on their neighbor's melons?"

Steven forgot about the guard entirely as he continued to ramble on.

"A kingdom without boundaries extends as far as the eye can see. And what difference if some other king sees the same thing? Come! Let us tear down all the boundary poles and bring them to the Prince as homage, bringing all that is rightfully his back to him." Steven was off searching for the next boundary pole. The guard, befuddled for a moment, soon followed him. Then in a burst of glee, ran ahead to the next pole and tore it down, taking the flag and rushing to the next pole some yards away. Steven watched, bemused, as the guard worked his way farther and farther up the boundary. Steven regained the road and continued his journey toward Rich Reach.

BY EVENING, STEVEN was rejoined by the guard, who showed him an entire bag full of flags and grinned as if he had a new puppy. The two made camp for the night and ate in companionable silence, though occasionally, Steven thought he heard the guard talking to himself.

"So, who are you, young revolutionary?" the guard asked Steven at last. "I will need to introduce you when we get to Rich Reach."

"I am Steven George the Dragonslayer," said Steven.

"Oh, that explains everything!" said the guard, nodding his head knowingly. "Father said things would change when the Dragonslayer got here. Father was certainly right about that!"

"Who is your father?" asked Steven George.

"Oh, that would be Montague Magnus the fourth, King and liege of Sylgale, Puissant Paragon of Mariria, and the Simple Pride of Arining," said the guard. "Also Lord Liege of Rich Reach, which he leaves in the hands of his less-than-shining son, Montague Valentine, Prince. Me."

"Oh! Your Majesty," Steven began. "Er... Royalness. Er... Princeliness," he continued. "I didn't know."

"Imagine that! He didn't know," laughed the Prince as if he were talking to another person at the fire. Steven looked carefully, but saw no one else. "I would be addressed as 'Your Highness' if we were being formal. But here we are, three companions camped in the woods, leading a revolution. You should call me Val. Only my closest friends call me Val," he said, nodding to his right. Steven looked again, but no one materialized.

"Yes, but Your Highness... I mean, Val," Steven sputtered, "what are you doing out here in the woods by yourself, dressed as a guard of the royal court and wearing a rock. I thought only the King's servants wore that symbol."

"And who would be more of a servant to the King than his son?" asked Val. "It is tradition that the crown prince will wear the symbol of servitude until the day he ascends the throne, thus marking him as a man of the people, so they will know him when he is their king."

"But why do you wander out here alone?" Steven asked.

"Oh, I'm not alone!" Val laughed. Steven looked around again. "I'm with you!" Then Val looked around himself. "You keep looking like someone else has appeared near me. Is there someone else around?" Val whispered.

"No, Your... Val," Steven answered. "But I was not with you when you came out here. Sergeant Busker taught me that soldiers never travel alone."

"Well, that would be the truth of it, if it weren't absolutely necessary," Val sighed. "The Terror has the people so frightened that once inside the city of Rich Reach, they refuse to leave. That includes the guards, who actually have all they can do to keep order in the overcrowded conditions as it is. Someone had to come out and check the boundaries, and we were all that were left. Of course, now we understand that the mission was to take down the boundaries and expand the kingdom as King Alli did in the days of old. Father was very clever in sending you."

"I hope he is happy with the results," Steven sighed.

"I have been practicing ever since I got word that Father had summoned you," Val said proudly.

"Practicing what?" Steven asked.

"My story," Val said. "Father sent very specific instructions that if I was to find out anything of importance from you, I would need to tell you a story first. Are you ready?"

"Certainly," said Steven. "When we Once Upon a Time each other, we are both one story richer. Please tell me."

And so, Prince Valentine began his story.

26
The Closed Book

ONCE UPON A TIME, there lived a great and wise king named Augustus Horatio. He ruled his kingdom with justice and fairness, and during his reign, all the people prospered and the kingdom grew in wealth and happiness. In the sparkling palace, even servants sang as they did their tasks, proud to be part of the King's household.

But it was not always that way in the royal household, nor was it always a happy kingdom. The great and wise King Augustus was once the foolish Prince Augie. Prince Augie was known far and wide as the stupidest child ever born to the royal household. He was inept in battle, a buffoon in the dining room. His school work was almost unintelligible, as all the royal tutors had quit when he was a small child and dedicated themselves to copying old manuscripts in a remote monastery.

Prince Augie, you might assume, was a prankster and problem child. But that would be a mistake. He was not clever enough to think up pranks, nor to think up ways to be a problem. It was enough that he existed and it was worse that he was his parents' only child, so one day would surely ascend to the throne. The whole kingdom despaired of the day when that would happen.

"Whatever shall we do?" moaned Augie's father as he watched his son pile blocks on top of each other in the nursery.

Augie was then sixteen summers old and the only task he could do successfully was build small buildings with the blocks in the nursery. Augie's mother let a tear fall as she looked at the child and squeezed her husband's arm.

"There is no choice," said his mother. "He is sixteen summers old and must prove himself worthy of the throne. He must be sent on a quest."

Both parents then wept, for they loved their stupid son and felt certain a quest would be the death of him. Yet it had to be done and so they sat in council to determine what quest they would set their son about.

"He should slay a dragon," said the minister of the army. "Only then will people believe that he is brave and clever enough to rule them."

"There has not been a dragon in this country in centuries," said the minister of farming. "It would be senseless to send him on such a quest. He should be sent to retrieve a rare fruit from a mountain lake guarded by a sea monster. He would have to show his cleverness by outwitting the monster and show his care for the people by bringing back a new source of food."

There were nods from around the table until the minister of literature spoke up.

"Rare fruits are only revealed when there is some dire emergency, according to the stories," said the minister of literature. "Someone must be dying and need a drop of dew from the mystical flower or some such, or there is no point in the quest."

"It makes no difference," said the King. "None of these things would be possible for my son. I will only accept a quest that is within reason for a lad of his… er… experience."

That caused a great silence to fall on the council chamber as everyone tried to think of a task that was within his grasp.

"It's no use," said the minister of the army at last. "We can scarcely send him to the market to fetch an egg. No one would believe that was a great enough task to prove his worth as a king."

"Ah," said the minister of literature, "but a simple task might be made to look much more difficult. We should send him to Quentin Renault." There was great silence. Quentin Renault had been the last of Prince Augie's tutors who fled to the monastery over four years ago, frustrated over his inability to teach the young prince.

"And why would this be a worthy quest?" asked the minister of farming. "Is it simply to find a man who does not want to be found by the boy?"

"No," said the minister of literature. "Actually, it is because Master Renault took one of my favorite books with him to copy at the monastery. He promised to return it soon, but I fear now that I shall never see it again. Prince Augie should be sent to the monastery to retrieve this rare book and bring it back to the royal library where it belongs."

"I fail to see how that shows his cleverness or his bravery," said the minister of the army. "It is still gathering eggs from the market."

"Yes," said the minister of literature, "but the pen is mightier than the sword. It will take Prince Augie several weeks to make his way to the monastery and back. In the meantime, we can create adventures that he 'might' have had and send them back on his behalf. Each week, we will gather the people to read the latest missive that will tell of

Prince Augie's great adventures. By the time he returns, he will be a great hero in the eyes of the people and they will be ready to accept him as their crown prince."

The King and Queen were pleased with this solution. The journey to the monastery was a long one into remote mountains, but it was comparably safe. And so it was decided.

On the sixteenth anniversary of the Prince's naming day, there was a great celebration. Musicians played all the prince's favorite music. Cooks prepared all the prince's favorite food. When the feast had been prepared and all had eaten, the King called his son before him. The ministers of literature, farming, and the army were called forth to describe the majesty of the quest that Prince Augie was to undertake.

"Our son," said the King, "is preparing to take his place as rightful heir to the throne." There were some groans among the people at these words, but Prince Augie assumed they were because the people had eaten too much. "As is traditional," the King continued, "he shall undertake a quest of great danger and worth."

The minister of the army then rose to speak at the King's command.

"Prince Augustus Horatio," the minister began.

There were some twitters of laughter among the audience, who had seldom heard the prince's full name unless he was being reprimanded by someone for an act of foolishness. Augie found the use of his full name to be funny as well, so the audience's laughter did not bother him.

"You will be given a horse and armor as a knight of the kingdom. You will undertake a perilous journey into the mountains to regain a valuable talisman that was lost to this kingdom some years ago. You will use whatever means you must to get this object from its current owner and return with it here."

Prince Augie was less than excited about how this sounded and was ready to bow out when the minister of literature rose to speak.

"For many years," the minister said, "there has been a book in the royal library that contains the wisdom and judgments of all the kings. Our kings have always ruled wisely because they had the *Book of Kings* on which to rely. This book was stolen from the library and must be returned. With this book, you will be able to rule wisely when it is time for you to inherit your father's throne."

It suddenly didn't sound so bad. Augie had gotten books from the library before and it didn't seem to be any great challenge. They had mostly been picture books. Then the minister of farming stood to speak.

"*The Book of Kings* was spirited away to the mountain monastery," said the minister of farming. "It holds the secrets to good husbandry that have always assured us of bountiful crops and healthy animals. Now enemies of the Kingdom might use *The Book of Kings* to hurt our harvests if they get to it first. The well-being of our kingdom depends on you bringing *The Book of Kings* back from the mountain monastery to the safety of the royal library."

Augie didn't like the sound of enemies trying to get the same thing he was going after, but he comforted himself by believing it was really only a trip to the library, and he would get to visit with some of his former tutors. He had always liked his tutors and did not understand why they became so frustrated with him. He had, after all, only asked a few simple questions.

And so it was that Prince Augie, dressed in shining armor and riding a white charger, was cheered as he rode out of the city gates on the road to the mountain monastery.

Now it so happened that there were spies at the royal banquet from an enemy nation. They had never before heard of the mysterious book that contained all the secrets of the kingdom.

"If we were to get this book before the foolish prince," they said among themselves, "then we could control their crops and invade their weakest places." They determined that they would capture the prince and use him as a hostage to demand the book from the monastery.

It was only a few days after the prince left the castle that the spies sprang their trap. Prince Augie was riding along near dusk, looking for a place to camp, when the spies fell upon him. Augie's horse was well-trained by the minister of the army and reared up to face the attack. Augie's visor fell over his eyes and he could not see as the horse turned and charged down the road past the enemy.

Augie let the horse go as he struggled to raise his visor so he could see. When he succeeded, he discovered the horse had turned off the road and was following a stream, the spies close behind. Ahead of Augie there appeared a stone bridge across the stream and his horse was headed straight for the arched opening through which ran the stream.

"Duck!" yelled Augie to himself, and since he had given the command himself, he immediately obeyed it and flattened himself on his horse's neck as the great beast charged beneath the bridge. The spies, following so closely behind that the spray of the horse's hooves blocked their vision, were knocked from their mounts as they ran beneath the bridge. They lay unconscious in the stream as

Augie and his horse continued to run down the stream and then back to the road toward the mountain monastery.

Back at the castle, the minister of literature had prepared the first 'report from the prince' to read to the people, without knowing what had occurred on the road.

"Spies attacked the prince on the road to the mountain monastery," the missive read. "In spite of being outnumbered three to one, Prince Augustus Horatio acquitted himself with deeds of bravery. The sun reflected from his shining armor and his gleaming sword as he beat the spies into submission. Then, showing his compassion and sense of justice, the Prince spared their lives, accepted their pledge of homage, and continued on his quest. Our Prince has shown himself brave in the face of grave danger and has brought honor and power to our country."

People had a bit of difficulty believing the Prince Augie they knew could have done this, but there it was in black and white. What else should they believe? And so, they nodded their heads and allowed a little bit of pride in their young prince to seep into their hearts.

Now, it happened as the sun shone on Prince Augie's shining armor, the inside of the armor got very hot. Augie's horse was unhappy about the heat as well, because white chargers also wear a great deal of armor. So, being a kind rider, Augie determined to help the horse. He came to a field in which the farmer, battling a ceaseless war against birds eating his crops, had erected a scarecrow. It happened that it was beside this scarecrow that Augie stopped to remove his oven-hot armor, and that of his horse.

As Augie got rid of his armor, he thought to himself that he couldn't really ride in just his linens. Besides, he was sore from the ride so far. He saw the scarecrow, dressed in ragged peasant's clothes. Quick as a wink, he stripped the scarecrow and donned its clothes, then put his armor on the scarecrow. Thinking that the proud figure of the scarecrow would look better astride a horse, he found a hay bale and dressed it in his horse's armor. The scarecrow looked much better now. Even the crows seemed to pay more respect to the shining armor the scarecrow now wore.

Augie began to walk, leading the charger. He was much too sore to ride. Just then, he saw a man with a draft horse pulling a cart.

"My, what a fine horse you have," said the farmer.

"Yes, but I am too sore from riding him," answered the prince. "I do wish I had a fine cart and horse like you have."

Now, the farmer thought this would be an easy simpleton to play a trick on, so he said, "This is a noble beast and the cart has served me for many years. If you had my cart and horse, noble sir, how would I then get around?"

"I know!" Augie replied. "Why don't we trade? I'll give you my white charger if you will give me your horse and cart."

It was almost too easy, thought the farmer, but he quickly made the trade and rode off on the charger laughing, "Simpleton!" as he rode away.

Prince Augie was ecstatic. He had a fine draft horse and a cart to ride in that was not as uncomfortable as the hard saddle of his charger.

He had not gone far, however, when he met a war party from his country's enemy. Having been told by the bedraggled spies about the clever prince, the enemy king had sent a raiding party of experienced soldiers to capture the prince. The enemy soldiers stopped in front of Prince Augie. He was very frightened.

"We are looking for a man in shining armor riding a great charger," said the leader of the raiding party. "Have you seen such a man?"

"Oh yes," said Prince Augie. "There is such a man just up the road in a cornfield battling a flock of crows!"

The raiders thought the prince was a simpleton and rode to find the man in armor. Augie put the whip to his horse and was far away when he heard the distant echo of a clash of steel as the raiding party attacked the scarecrow.

BACK AT THE castle, the minister of literature released the second 'report from the prince'—a fine work of fiction he had written himself.

"Prince Augustus Horatio was attacked by a horde of enemy soldiers seeking to prevent his quest. The Prince battled nobly and struck down many of the soldiers. But ultimately, the odds were too great against him."

The people gasped to think their prince had been harmed.

"But," continued the minister, "our prince had befriended a kindly spirit along the way and that spirit came to the Prince's aid. He was said to have vanished. So, all the soldiers found were pieces of armor as the prince was spirited away into the mountains."

The people of the Kingdom were astounded at the news, and when soldiers, sent out to check on the prince came upon the raiding party, they were astounded to find only the prince's armor and a story that he had vanished from their midst.

AND SO IT went as the Prince continued his journey. He had few adventures, but the minister of literature released a new missive each week telling how he mastered a sphinx's riddle, tricked an ogre, and slew a dragon. The people of the Kingdom began to gather early on the day that a new episode was due and shake their heads in wonder that the simple prince had been able to master so many challenges on his quest.

At last, without any great problem, Prince Augie arrived at the mountain monastery and asked to see Master Quentin Renault. He found the scholar sitting in front of the fire. An insect was dragging a glass of sherry across the table next to the tutor. Prince Augie bravely strode to the tableside and squashed the bug.

"Oh no!" cried Master Renault. "Not you! Do you know how long it has taken me to train that dung beetle to bring me my drink?"

"You taught a dung beetle to retrieve?" asked Augie. "that is amazing!" He wiped the remains of the insect from his sword.

"It was easier than teaching you!" the master exclaimed.

"However did you do it?" asked the prince.

"I had the book," Master Renault said. "I suppose you have come for it now."

"Yes," said Augie. "I am prepared to do battle with you for possession if necessary, and complete my quest to return the book to its place in the royal library."

"You needn't do battle," said the scholar. "Just take it and be gone. You've caused enough trouble in my life." He pointed at a book that rested closed on a reading table.

"Will this book teach me to train a dung beetle?" the prince asked in awe as he picked up the heavy volume.

"Yes," said the scholar, "and how to be a good king. It will teach you how to make the crops plentiful and how to keep your enemies at bay."

Augie hefted the book and tried to open it, causing himself to lose control of the massive volume and drop it to the floor. The master groaned.

"It's locked," said Augie.

"Of course it is locked," said the master. "You can never understand what is in the book unless you hold the key." With that the scholar pulled a long cord from around his neck, at the end of which was a large key. This he draped around Augie's neck. "There, now you hold the key."

"So now I can unlock the book and read all its secrets!" the Prince exclaimed.

"Pisshhh," the master declared. "You don't need to read it if you hold the key to the book. Just having it is all you need. When you get back to the castle, you will find that you have all that you need to rule the kingdom well. Just continue to be a kind and simple person," Master Quentin Renault said gently. Then resuming his irascible temperament, he said, "Now go! Get out of here before you kill my cook, as well!"

"Do you have a dung beetle that cooks for you?" asked Prince Augie in surprise.

"No, of course not," said Master Quentin. "Dung beetles are terrible cooks. It is the queen honeybee that makes my meals!" With no more hospitality than that, the master ushered Augie to the door and sent him home.

THE YOUNG PRINCE had an equally uneventful trip back to the castle, but when he was still some days away, he was met by a man riding a fine white charger.

"You there," said the man pulling up beside the cart. "This horse has been nothing but trouble for me since we traded. I demand that you give me back my own horse and cart and take your foul-tempered stallion back."

Augie was reluctant, but the farmer was justified in that he really couldn't use a war horse on the farm to haul his hay, so Augie agreed to the change.

As it happened, word had found its way back to the enemy kingdom that Augie had traded his warhorse and armor and the enemy king sent another raiding party after the prince. This raiding party met Augie on the road and stopped him.

"You there!" demanded the leader. "We are looking for a ragged man with a horse and cart that was to be on this road. Have you seen such a one?"

"Why yes," said the prince. "He is not more than two leagues behind me."

At that the raiding party rode off at a gallop and the prince trotted on toward the castle. In a field not far away, he found his armor. It was scuffed and bent and not so shiny. There was no sign of the scarecrow. But Prince Augie put on the armor the best he could manage, armored his horse, and jangled on toward the castle.

PEOPLE WERE LINING the battlements to watch as Prince Augustus Horatio finally approached the castle. His horse clumped across the bridge. Looking at the people, the prince held up the book that he brought from the mountain monastery and all the people cheered. He rode proudly to the market square where he had begun his journey. There he met his mother and father and the gathered council of ministers. For the first time in his life, Prince Augustus felt successful as he delivered the great book to the minister of literature. The King then spoke.

"This is my son!" he declared to the crowd. They cheered loudly. "Prince Augustus Horatio, you have taken on a great quest and you have returned successful. You have faced enemy soldiers, spies, wild animals, and desolate roads. And you have returned successful! It is my great pride to bestow upon you the rank of Crown Prince and heir to the throne. After me, you will rule wisely and our kingdom will prosper."

The people cheered again.

It was some time before Prince Augustus heard the stories that had been told about his adventures on his miraculous quest. When he heard them, they seemed right to him. He thought that truly must have been what happened, because it was right there in black and white.

When his father and mother were old and on their deathbeds, his father blessed him and Augustus became King Augustus Horatio. All the people expected him to be wise and just, and so, all that he did appeared to be so. And under his rule, the Kingdom prospered.

The book was never opened. King Augustus held the key, and that was all that was necessary.

27
Prince

IN THE MORNING, Steven and Prince Val continued to the City and Castle of Rich Reach. The Prince carried on a lively conversation as they walked—sometimes with Steven. As they traveled, the Prince continued to pull down boundary markers and to collect their flags. Sometimes, the talk was of the banished Terror, and at others about the tasks of governing such a large principality. At times, it seemed the prince was giving instructions to unseen minions for preparing a welcome and banquet for Steven. Steven constantly caught himself looking for whoever it was the Prince was talking to, but there was never anyone present.

"Now, about the Terror," said the Prince as they walked. "You say it was really just the thief called Ibin Ariaga who was terrorizing people with stories and secretly going out and moving the boundary markers?"

"Yes," said Steven. "The villagers of Alinata are holding him awaiting your pleasure."

"That will never do," said the prince.

"Do you want me to go back and fetch him?" Steven asked.

"Great heavens, no!" exclaimed the prince. "I'll send guards to arrest him properly. The story of the thief terrorizing the entire kingdom is what will not do. We must have a Terror that you have conquered. Let me see. A monster that you have slain, perhaps? No, no, he would have to bring back the head or ears or some proof if he had slain a monster." Steven once again realized that he was now subject of a conversation that did not include him, so remained silent while the prince continued.

"A being of the spirit world, then? Or a witch that dissolved in a puddle of water? Dust! That is it! A corpse that turned to dust when the dragonslayer slew it! Again. There are so many possible terrors. What do you think?" asked the Prince.

Steven waited for the Prince to continue until he realized that the Prince had actually turned to him for an opinion. Clearing his throat, Steven meekly asked, "Why not the truth?"

"Storyteller," the Prince began, "I do not want my entire kingdom humiliated by believing that the Terror was no more than a prankster. You would be no hero and the people would think they were idiots. People who do not believe in themselves cannot be productive and profitable. The entire economy would collapse. Now if we were to collect enough dust for it to be plausible that it was a corpse, we could dole it out gradually to the souvenir vendors who could sell it at a handsome price. Whenever people begin to doubt themselves, we could put a little more Terror Dust on the market and there would be a revival. We must make people believe there was a real, monstrous Terror; they were right to be afraid; and we have a true hero in our midst who has saved us from said Terror. Then the people will return to their homes in confidence to rebuild. They will find no encroaching boundary markers. They will know that the kingdom is safe as far as the eye can see, and they will be happy."

"But that would be a lie," said Steven sadly.

"No," said the Prince. "It would be a story."

The two walked on in silence for a distance—a remarkable feat for the Prince. Soon they were in sight of the castle parapets and the Prince stopped to address Steven directly before they entered.

"The answer is in the book," said the prince with confidence. "But since the answer must finally come from you, it is you who must use the book. I will give you the key, and you will tell me the answer the book gives you."

"You mean there really are a book and a key?" Steven asked in amazement.

"As surely as there is a sheepskin vest on your back," answered the Prince. "Here is the key. You will have uninterrupted time in the library before the feast tonight, and you will find the answer and bring it to us." With that, the Prince removed a cord from around his neck with a key at the end. "Get that back to me as soon as possible," the Prince directed. "I feel foolish without it."

THE ENTRY INTO Rich Reach was heroic. People lined the streets to greet their Prince and Steven, who was more than a little embarrassed. It *did* almost appear that the Prince had communicated with the castle staff before their arrival, since all arrangements had been made for the great feast later that night. Steven was taken to a chamber to freshen up, and then led to the library where "the book" was kept.

"Does the Prince come here often?" asked Steven of his librarian guide.

"Oh yes, sir," answered the librarian. "It seems he is always in here. That's why no one else ever uses the library."

"I beg your pardon? Doesn't the Prince let others use the library?" asked Steven.

"Oh, he does not object," said the librarian. "But with the Prince in here, it is already crowded." Steven looked around the large chamber, but could imagine how just the Prince could seem like a crowd. He was led to the book and the librarian retired.

The lock on the book was ancient and rusty. It hadn't been opened in many years and the key did not turn on the first try. Steven reached in his pocket and found the oil-skin that had wrapped his duck sandwich. It was smeared in duck fat, and he applied some of this to the lock and to the key. After a time of working the key back and forth, the lock popped open and Steven pried the cover back from the first page of the ancient book.

It was blank.

Steven flipped through page after page of the great book, but all were blank. Steven smiled and then chuckled. He finally laughed out loud. He knew the story he would tell at the banquet. He relocked the book and went to the great chamber where the Prince was waiting with many actual people of the court in attendance. Steven returned the key, and after they had eaten their meal, he rose to tell his story.

28
The Terror Within

ONCE UPON A TIME, a great coldness fell upon the Village of Last Hope. It was not the coldness of winter. It was not the coldness of snow or ice. It was not the coldness of a forsaken lover. It was a coldness that chilled the heart and made the spine tingle. It was a coldness that raised bumps on the arms and sent chills down the neck. It was a coldness such that it made men's blood run cold in their veins.

This coldness came because the Village of Last Hope lay in the shadow of the great and ancient dragon Malzath.

You have probably heard of Malzath. It was he who nested in the peaks of the Zathron Mountains. It was he who had scorched the earth of the South so that nothing was left but desert sands. It was he who froze the peaks of the mountains so the snow never melted. When he spread his wings to fly, great hurricanes swept the coasts of the seas. When he stomped in anger, the entire earth shook beneath his feet.

And the people of Last Hope dwelt in his shadow.

In truth, Malzath had never had an issue with the people of Last Hope. He scarcely knew they existed, but the people were terrified of him nonetheless. He was a great and terrible dragon, capable of devouring their little village in a single bite. With one claw he could open a rift in the earth that would swallow them whole. The fear of Malzath increased to the point that people began to whisper among themselves that something had to be done about Malzath.

When people live in the shadow of fear, grave things begin to happen. It began as the village council met. As the Elder stood to speak, a young man stood up and shouted, "What are you going to do about Malzath?" At once, the council house was filled with chaos as anger took root amidst the fear.

When he had regained some control, the elder spoke calmly and reassuringly. "There is nothing to be done about Malzath. If we simply ignore him, he will continue to ignore us. Let us not awaken the sleeping dragon."

But the people were not happy with this answer. They called the elder weak. They said he had no principles. They even accused the elder of being in league with the dragon, plotting the downfall of the Village of Last Hope. They rebelled against the elder and drove him out of the village. Cast out, without hope or sustenance, the elder became a wandering pilgrim searching for the meaning of life.

WITHOUT AN ELDER to lead them, the villagers turned to the shaman. "What shall we do about Malzath?" they demanded.

With no elder, the fear had grown among the people. Without a leader, they were blind and willing to follow anyone's lead. But the shaman had learned from the example of the elder and declined to follow the wise course. Knowing the volatility of the people, he offered his solution timidly.

"Perhaps we should offer a sacrifice to Malzath," the shaman said. "We will appease his anger and he will look kindly on us."

This seemed like a good thing to the people of Last Hope. If they pleased the dragon, surely, he would leave them alone. And so the day of sacrifice was set.

The people of Last Hope were excited about the new plan up until the very moment when they staked a poor young boy to the mountain where they thought Malzath would find him. When the deed had been done, the people were saddened and filled with remorse. When they went to rescue the boy, he was gone. They turned their anger and guilt on the shaman and drove him from the village. The shaman fled with his life and became a hermit in a far-off forest.

The people next turned to the village wise woman. She, having seen what happened to the elder and the shaman, offered no solution, but slipped out of the village that night and became an itinerant midwife for the villages on the far side of the river.

And the people of Last Hope still dwelt in the shadow of Malzath.

At last, there was a whisper. No one knew who started it, but soon the whisper turned to a rumor and the rumor to a decision.

"We must," declared the people, "slay the dragon."

The village came together, young and old, and decided the best way to choose who should slay the dragon would be to draw lots. An equal number of black and of white stones were placed in a pot and all the people of the village drew out a stone. Those who had white stones prepared the pebbles for the second round of the lottery with an equal number of black and white stones. Those who had drawn black stones in the first round drew again in the second round. This was repeated until only ten people had drawn black stones in the penultimate round. Then, ten stones were put in the pot—nine white and one black. The last ten people drew their final stone.

It was a maiden who drew the black pebble.

Now, this maiden was not the strongest person in the village. Neither was she the smartest of all the people. Nor was she particularly clever. But she was fair-minded, and having drawn the black lot, she was content to go out to slay the dragon.

She was armed as best the village could arm her. She was provisioned as well as the village could provide. And on a day of great celebration, the village sent their Last Hope Champion out to do battle with the dragon.

"Do not fear," said the maiden. "I will slay the dragon and then I will go on to see the world. If you never see me again, you will know that I was successful."

And so, she set off on her adventure.

As she left the village, the people noticed already that it was a little less cold. They had sent a champion to do what none of them felt able to do. And every day she was gone, the hope increased and the coldness of the shadow lessened. When she had not returned in a year, the people began to nod their heads and smiles appeared. When she had been gone for seven years, people began to celebrate. When she had been gone for twenty years, people had begun to forget about the dragon, and the coldness of heart had been lifted from the Village of Last Hope.

As for their champion, she soon discovered that she did not really know what a dragon looked like. She did not know how to slay it if she found it. And it was not likely that she would find it, since she did not know precisely where it lived. So, she began a pilgrimage that took her all across the earth, but never closer to her dragon.

Now as it happened, the maiden wandered and met a man who fell in love with her. Since she could not and would not stay with him, he wandered with her. He dressed in a simple shepherd's manner with leather trousers and a sheepskin vest. He was pleasant company for the maiden.

He was stronger than she, but the two together were formidable. So, when a band of brigands fell upon them, they drew their swords and chased them off. So great was their rage that the brigands were never seen on that road again.

In a city, when they were about to be cheated by a merchant, they united to right the situation. So swift was their justice that merchants in that city have been honest ever since.

When she wept with sorrow for her village, he comforted her. When she danced with joy, he sang. When she smiled at him he wept with joy.

When the maiden dragonslayer was very old, he laid her to rest where her ashes could nourish the crops and his tears would water them.

Some say, when she died, he went far into the mountains and was never heard of again. Others say he wanders the roads yet to this day, wearing his shepherd's clothes and telling stories of things that might have been.

But what is certain is the Village of Last Hope has never been under the cold shadow of Malzath since. Nor shall you ever again fear the Terror, for the shepherd now walks among you.

29
What the Sergeant Didn't See

STEVEN GEORGE BOWED to the people of Rich Reach and bowed to Prince Montague Valentine.

"All this was in the book?" Val asked Steven.

"You need never know what is in the book," Steven answered. "Only that it is there."

The Prince pushed a bundle toward Steven across the banquet table. It was long and slender. As Steven unwrapped it, both a dagger and a sword fell out. Each had a delicately carved hilt that fit Steven's hand perfectly. But more amazingly, on the blades were engraved the figures of two dragons. The engravings glowed with a light of their own and if they were turned just right, one might see the figure of a lady on the sword and of a child on the dagger. Steven smiled.

"If I may, Your Highness," Steven said to the Prince, "I should like a bit of fresh air. May I walk on the battlements?"

"By all means, Steven George the Dragonslayer," said Prince Valentine. He addressed the people gathered at the banquet, who were still whispering among themselves over Steven's story.

"May all the people know that Steven George the Dragonslayer has met and mastered the Terror of Rich Reach, and we are ever thankful for the safety that this ensures for our kingdom and our people. Wherever he goes, he is the emissary of the King and friend of the Prince. There are no boundaries to the protection that he provides." And so, having shaken the Prince's hand and embraced as true friends, Steven left the banquet hall.

LATE AT NIGHT, the Prince decided to see if Steven was still on the battlements, for he had not seen him since the feast. He saw many guards scurrying about the palace, looking in corners and behind rusty suits of armor. He hurried on to the castle wall.

"Well, there is no reason he should stay here, is there?" the Prince said. "He fulfilled his task."

"But how could he leave the castle with the gates all closed for the night?" the Prince answered.

"Perhaps you should ask the Sergeant," the Prince said.

"Sergeant, where is the Dragonslayer?" the Prince demanded.

"Now, Your Grace, we'd all like to know that. He was here some time ago," the Sergeant answered.

THE SERGEANT HAD not always been a sergeant, of course. He had begun his career as a lowly yeoman and survived enough battles to rise to the top of his ranks. The Sergeant learned many things in his career. When the commanding officer gave an order, he obeyed. Instantly. When he was asked a question, he answered. Clearly. And when he was given a troop to lead, he led. Courageously.

But perhaps the most important thing the Sergeant learned was how to communicate with both his superiors and his men. He discovered that what he did not say was as important as what he did say.

"Sergeant!" yelled the Captain. Captains always yelled and thus when sergeants spoke to their troops, they yelled as well. This was the first lesson in communication. Whispers were for spies. Soldiers yelled. "Did you see any enemy troops coming over that ridge?"

"No sir!" the Sergeant yelled back at the Captain. "I saw enemy troops coming through the forest over there."

"I know about the enemy in the forest," yelled the Captain. "I asked you about the enemy on the ridge."

"Yes sir!" yelled the Sergeant.

"Yes sir, you saw enemy troops coming over the ridge?"

"No sir! I saw no enemy troops coming over the ridge, sir."

"Dismissed!"

The Sergeant left the Captain's tent having learned a valuable lesson. Answer only the question you are asked. It seemed to make sense. The next time the Sergeant was called before the Captain to report, the Captain barked, "Sergeant! Has the supply wagon arrived?"

"Yes sir," the Sergeant responded. He did not add that the wagon was empty and the escort was gone. The Captain found out soon enough.

You might think that not giving all the knowledge one has when asked a question would be counter-productive, but it served the Sergeant well through his career. The Captain knew he could count on a clear and concise answer to the question he asked, and not have his time wasted with other details. And he could always ask more questions to get additional information if he needed it. This went well until the Sergeant discovered a particularly important (to him) bit of information that the Captain really needed in order to succeed in the campaign.

"Sergeant!" barked the Captain. "How many enemy are coming through the forest?"

"None sir," the sergeant yelled.

"And how many are coming over the ridge?"

"None sir."

"Then we are done here. Sound the retreat," yelled the Captain. Now it happened that the Sergeant had seen a large party of the enemy coming at them from behind—in fact, from the direction of their retreat. He puzzled for a moment before he announced his information.

"I am not saying I saw no enemy coming from behind us," he bellowed.

"How many enemy are you not saying are coming from behind?" asked the Captain.

"I'm not saying there are 400 troops coming from behind, sir. Nor am I saying they are armed with bows and lances."

"And what else are you not saying?" yelled the Captain.

"I'm not saying that I miss my wife and children, sir."

"Good! Sound the charge and lead the men over the ridge!" And so it happened that the Sergeant learned that what he was not saying could be as important as what he was saying, but not to push it.

His ability to communicate stood him in good stead when he was off the battle field as well. Take for instance, his wife's new dress. Like good soldierly wives, she was hearty and stout and he loved her dearly, but she was a bit vain, which he tolerated amiably. One day she approached her husband to show him the new dress she was wearing.

"Don't you just love this new dress?" Mrs. Sergeant shouted at her husband.

"I can't say that it isn't the loveliest dress I never seen," bellowed her husband.

"You don't think it makes my hips look big, do you?" she yelled.

"I haven't never seen nothing that doesn't make your hips look big like this doesn't," he answered. Then he quickly excused himself to return to his platoon for six months active duty abroad.

None of which is what this story is about.

During a peaceful season, before the Sergeant was sent to manage the troops at Rich Reach, he had been in charge of the guard that patrolled the parapets of the King's palace. You might think it strange that the parapets would be guarded during a time of peace, but you have to have something to keep soldiers occupied or they start thinking about becoming farmers. In order to keep the soldiers occupied and alert on their rounds, every slight provocation or rumor was used as an excuse to double the guards.

"A sheep has been stolen, sir!" reported a scout.

"Double the guards!" yelled the Sergeant.

"A wolf is prowling the outlying farms, sir!" the Sergeant reported to the Captain.

"Double the guards!" the Captain yelled at once.

"A stranger is approaching the castle gates!" a page called out.

"Double the guards!" the King shouted at the Captain.

But, of course, the wolf who stole the sheep had been killed by a farmer. A traveling minstrel, dressed in the skin of the wolf as a gift from the farmer, was bringing the story to the castle, so the guards returned to their barracks.

Thus, it happened that the Sergeant knew how to address his Prince.

"SERGEANT, WHERE IS the Dragonslayer?" the Prince demanded.

"Now, Your Grace, we'd all like to know that. He was here some time ago," the Sergeant answered.

"Are you saying he just disappeared?" bellowed the Prince.

"I am saying, Your Highness," explained the Sergeant of the Night Watch, "that I saw Master Dragonslayer mount the battlement after the banquet last night—and that was a fine story he told, was it not?—and that we never saw him come down. I am not saying he disappeared, only that he cannot be found in the castle or the City of Rich Reach."

"And he is gone without a trace?" asked the bemused prince.

"Now I am not saying that he left without a trace," said the Sergeant. "There is this here sheepskin vest that was just lying up there on the battlements. We thought as Your Highness might like to have it, to sort of keep for when he was found."

"Sergeant," bellowed the Prince as if speaking to a battalion. "How came this sheepskin to be here?"

"It came in the company of the Dragonslayer your majesty entertained last evening, sire."

"And where is the Dragonslayer now?" demanded the Prince again, looking in every direction.

"I can't say, Your Highness," said the Sergeant.

"Why not?"

"Soldiers don't tell stories," the Sergeant answered. "Soldiers say only what they see with their own two eyes. Soldiers must always be depended upon to report accurately to their superior officers."

"I'm not asking for a story," bellowed the Prince. "I am asking for your report."

"Yes, Sire. The Dragonslayer mounted the battlements wearing sheepskin vest. I'm not saying I didn't see him drop the vest when he seemed to see a dragon that wasn't sitting on the parapet opposite the tower. I cannot say he didn't reach out to the dragon that wasn't there, nor that at not touching it, the Dragonslayer didn't sprout wings on his back and didn't mount into the sky on the non-existent wings, nor did he fly away with the dragon who wasn't there, so obviously did not mount into the sky with the Dragonslayer who didn't have wings." The Sergeant paused to draw a breath, but the Prince interrupted him.

"You saw a dragon?"

"I didn't say that."

"Is there anything else you didn't see?"

"I didn't see flames not dripping from his mouth as he didn't fly," said the Sergeant.

"So, the Dragonslayer just disappeared without a trace?" the Prince asked.

"Well, I wouldn't say without a trace, Your Highness, as there is the sheepskin vest lying here on the battlement."

"And you don't know where the Dragonslayer went?" the Prince asked one last time.

"I can say with absolute certainty that the Dragonslayer in question is right here on this very battlement no more," the Sergeant said.

"Thank you for your clear report, Sergeant," the Prince said.

"It's all in learning to communicate, Sire," the Sergeant answered.

The Prince put on the sheepskin vest and was amazed to find it fit him so well. He remembered Steven as being somewhat smaller than he was. But the vest fit quite well. He even felt more princely when wearing it. When he put his hand in the pocket, he found a leather thong with a rock tied to the end of it. He wondered what else he might find in the pockets.

"I see," said the Prince as he looked into the night sky and smiled. He stuck a hand in his pocket and pulled out three balls. He started tossing them in the air and soon was able to keep them all flying from hand to hand. He chuckled.

"The shepherd walks among you," he mused as he tugged at the vest.

"I guess you know what that means," he answered himself.

"What was that, Your Highness?" asked the Sergeant.

"Was I talking to you?" asked the Prince.

"I… ah… As you wish, Sire," said the Sergeant.

"Carry on," responded the Prince as he walked away.